FIND ME

DANGEROUS ENTANGLEMENTS

ANNE ROMAN

La Noir Media, LLC

CHAPTER ONE

Simon

"Honey badger come, come in honey badger." The radio tucked into my low visibility armor kit crackled to life. I ignored it, just like I ignored the tingling itch of sweat dripping down the back of my neck into the moisture-soaked keffiyeh. The neck scarf was supposed to protect me from the dust and dirt that seemed to coat everything in this god-forsaken country, but on days like today, when the sun beat down on us in waves, all it did was add another layer of irritation to erode my already shitty mood.

I'd been tucked into the side of a mountain in the southern mountain ranges of Syria for going on two days and would be there for several more if necessary. It all depended on when and if the intel U.S. forces had shared with us was accurate. And they typically were. The radio crackled to life again. "Honey badger, please respond."

There was a movement of rock next to me, a shift so subtle few would have noticed it. But I was trained to know when my partner moved even a minuscule inch, and they had the same training.

"You better answer him." My eyes slid towards the blur of brown and gray that blended seamlessly into the mountain terrain next to me. To anyone who stood even a few inches away from our location, it would have appeared as if the rocks themselves were talking.

"I'm not fecking answering. He can use my damn call sign."

"He's just going to keep on until you respond."

At that, the radio crackled to life again. "Honey- 'I snatched it from my kit and hit the transmitter.

"Call me fecking honey badger one more time E and I swear on my mother I'll cut your balls off and feed them to one."

There was a slight pause before a voice came across the radio again, only it wasn't Evan. "Reaper cut the shit. This is Colonel Smith. Have you seen any movement?"

A soft chuckle came from the rock pile next to me and I cut a glare towards it, clearing my throat. "Apologies sir, that's a negative. No movement on the southern ridge."

"Fine. Get to the extraction point. We need your team elsewhere."

I felt the tick of the muscles in my jaw as I clenched it

and took a few seconds to pause before I answered. "Sir, I think you should reconsider. We're already fully in place and ready to engage. The intel we received from the Americans said that this is the most likely route the target's men will be taking."

The same sharp voice came across the radio once more. "Your concerns are duly noted. However, we have other more pressing matters that need your expertise. Pack it up and get to the extraction point."

"Roger, Sir. Reaper out."

I barely heard the whisper of movement before I felt the light hand on my shoulder and glanced up at my partner. Her face was covered with brown and gray camouflage paint, but I could make out the sparkle of blue eyes that smiled down at me.

I stood, removing the rocks and pieces of a brittle shrub that helped me blend in with my environment

"What's so funny?"

There was a flash of white as she grinned and then turned away, beginning to pack up her gear and disassemble the high-powered rifle that would have left the brains of anyone within 500 yards a mere stain in the dirt.

"Oh, just thinking about our days in selection. Remember how we thought we were going to save the world?"

I snorted, helping her pack up the gear, before slinging the heavy ruck over my shoulders. After eight years of crossing mountainous terrain, icy slopes, and arid desserts, the weight of the pack felt familiar and comfortable. "I remember trying to get you to kiss me outside the slop tent when it was our turn on KP duty."

It was her turn to snort as she slung her own pack over her shoulders and I let her take the lead as we made our way down the mountainside. "Hmm... and do you need another reminder of what happened to you then?"

I grinned, "Tsk, come now my little trigger-happy tease, you wouldn't want to hurt your favorite part of me."

"You don't need your tongue for me to use my favorite part of you, Simon Gallagher."

We rounded a low cropping of boulders just as the wind around us picked up and the dove gray Osprey landed a few hundred yards from us in the hard-packed dirt.

"Och, well now, looks like I'm going to have to do my best to make my tongue you other favorite part of me." I grinned as she threw me an eye roll and then sprinted out from behind the boulders towards the waiting Osprey. I could just barely make out the words over the wind whipping around us from the whirling blades. "You'll have to catch me first!"

Simon

The cold slap of water on my face cut through the hazy fog of my dreams, and I woke up with a start. It took only seconds for reality to set in. A quick check of my extremities told me I was in the same position I'd been in for the last several days, strapped to a cold exam table with just a thin sheet covering my lower half. At least they left the sheet this time.

I swallowed past the dry ache in my throat, reminding me that I couldn't remember the last time I'd had anything to drink.

I tried to open my swollen eyes and turn towards where I thought the water had come from, but could only make out rough shapes. Shape one was large and hovered off to the side. Shape two was smaller and came closer as my head tried to angle towards it. Cold hands traced across my chest toward my ribs and I winced when they lingered over the bruises there. From the way the pain radiated sharply with every breath I inhaled, I was pretty sure a couple of them were broken.

"Did you love her?"

The soft voice pierced my ears, and I knew who was touching me now. Bile rose in my throat and it took all the willpower I had not to visibly recoil at the feel of her hand tracing languid patterns over my bruises. I knew better than to stay silent. However, it would only give her reason to continue to touch me.

"I don't know what yer talking about."

Her tongue clicked in soft disapproval. "Oh come now, Simon. You were moaning her name just now in your sleep. I wonder, does my sister know about your other lover? About our history?"

I winced as sharp nails gripped the tender edge of

one of my ribs, curling around it and digging in with slow and steady pressure.

"Ye know I loved her." I barked the words out with a hiss of pain, sweat pooling at my temples. I worried those fingers would continue to dig into me, but my answer seemed to surprise her and she pulled her hand away.

"*Did I?*" The slow, languid, petting began again. Her hand traced all the patterns of my beaten and bruised body.

"Aye, you knew. And she loved me until you poisoned her mind." I waited for the overwhelming sense of grief and rage to come whenever I spoke about Victoria, but it didn't. Instead, there was just a dull ache at the memory of the dream I'd been lost in.

"I think we remember things very differently." Fingernails trailed over open cuts on my skin and I hissed again at the sensation. The mix of soft caresses, almost sensual in the way she skimmed her fingers over my broken body, and the pain she inflicted at the same time, made me nauseated. "How did she die?"

The question was asked innocently enough, but I knew it was anything but. She leaned towards me, her eyes dilated and shining with intense interest, even though she maintained an emotionless expression.

"You should know. You killed her." The pain made my accent, so carefully cultivated to be hidden over the years so that I could blend in with the surrounding environment, spill across my busted lips in a rough brogue.

"Simon, poor Simon, all these years spent hunting me. Looking for revenge." A disappointed pout turned her full lips down and for a moment, I thought of another pair of pouty lips. "And yet you're still blaming someone else for your own mistakes. I wasn't the one who put the bullet in Tory's head."

"Oh, you did. You set up the meeting. You manipulated Tory into helping you all for a promise of money and riches. You might not have pulled the trigger, but you loaded the damn gun."

"Hmm...." was the only sound she made as she continued her inspection of every cut and bruise on my body.

I continued, ignoring the sickening sensation that traveled up my thighs to my gut as her nails dug into another deep gash. "I should have known. The way she talked about you." Emotions threatened to overwhelm me, but I'd be dammed if I let the evil bitch see it.

After the Colonel had pulled us back from our overwatch position, we'd learned that new intel had suggested that the leader of a local extremist sect had been tasked as the middleman to broker a deal between a new arms dealer and the caliphate. The chatter on some channels had indicated the dealer had come into possession of some new drone technology the Iranians had cultivated from captured U.S. drones. How they'd managed to get their hands on billions of dollars worth of tech like that blew my mind and part of me thought it was just a hoax. A distraction from the terrorist training camps they were building up in other areas.

When I'd grumbled to Tory about my lack of faith in our leadership, she'd just glared at me, her lips pressed together in a thin line of resentment. I knew that look. It was the look that came right before the "*I told you so.*"

It was an old argument between us. For the past couple of years, Victoria had grown more and more disgruntled with our line of work. And not just our work, but tedious toll that constant missions took on us. More than once, she'd mentioned that our necks were on the line for people who only ever sat behind a teleprompter and used our services to elevate their own positions. The conversation always made me uncomfortable. While we weren't sitting on stacks of cash, being off the record of any military unit in Her Majesty's service meant that we were paid handsomely for the risks we took. Not to mention the innocent lives we saved.

That was enough for me. Let politicians be the slime balls they typically were, so long as my conscious was clean and I felt like I was doing the right thing. But lately, Tory had wanted more. She'd begun talking about moving to privatized services and had even begun making contacts in some underground sectors for black-ops contractors. Mercenaries for hire, or worse.

"We're putting our necks out for pennies when we would could be doing half the work for three times the pay."

"Tory, you're asking me to betray my country, my unit, just for an easy pay day."

"Si.. come on, you know the minute we leave these weapons are just going to go right back into the hands of the people we're trying to keep them from. We're just wasting our time, our blood and sweat and tears for nothing. None of this matters in the end. We're just the pawns on their fucking chess-board. The most expendable pieces they have to play." Her blue *eyes pleaded with mine to believe her, to join her.*

Pain arched from the soles of my feet, and I snapped back to the present.

"You seem to have drifted away there, Simon." Sybil's eyes glinted in the room's dimness, a predator watching her prey. "You were just telling how Tory's death was my fault."

"Aye, you killed her. You sold her a lie, and it killed her."

Suddenly, nails like knives sank into the lacerations that crisscrossed my abdomen and I cried out in pain this time. My back and neck arched as the breath was snatched away from me and it left me gasping for air. Darkness clouded the edges of my vision and as I faded out of consciousness, I felt her hot breath against my ear. "Tory knew exactly what she was getting into. If anything, I gave her the chance to free herself from a life of lies. If anyone's lying, it's you, Simon. Don't twist the truth, I'm not the one with her blood on my hands, isn't that right... *Reaper?*"

CHAPTER TWO

Hannah

I looked down at the shiny black pumps on my feet and watched as if from a distance as they tapped a fast rhythm on the white and pristine marbled floor. The marble was so shiny I could just make out the red reflection of their bottoms. Whenever I felt I needed a little extra boost of confidence, I always went to my Louboutin's and if ever I needed that boost, it was today. Shifting in the stiff leather chair, I sighed and glanced up at the enormous clock on the wall just across from me. They say justice is patient, but somehow I must have missed that memo. Because all I could think was that with every tick of the clock, the seconds were eating at the distance between me and my sister. *And Simon.*

I felt a presence next to me like a dark shadow, but I didn't turn towards it. Ever since I'd agreed to help Rue locate Simon, either her, Micheal, or Evan had been a constant presence at my side. They'd insisted it was for my protection since the Abromov Group, or rather Sybil, would be targeting me, but it felt more like they were making sure I didn't back out of my end of the bargain.

And the bargain? I'd find Sybil and, in turn, locate Simon, but then Sybil was mine to deal with. They would get what they needed to shut down the weapons dealing portion of the Abromov Group, but I'd get my sister. And then I'd get my justice.

But first, I had to piece back together the shambles of my life that Sybil had destroyed. Starting with getting reinstated as an FBI agent and clearing my name.

Rubbing sweaty palms on the front of my slacks, I finally turned to look at the colossal figure, who was leveling me with his dark gaze. I'd thought Michael, and I had come to an understanding when we were in Switzerland, or at least, an easy camaraderie. But since the night at the gala, he'd been back to silently promising to kill me a hundred different ways with just a look.

It pissed me off.

What right did he have to be upset with me? He and the rest of the team had been just as guilty as Simon when they'd lied about their true intentions. But now he acted as if I was the enemy and he was just waiting for the chance to dump me off in the nearest ditch.

I stared right back at him and then slowly, as if I was pulling something from the pocket of my suit jacket, flipped him off. I could see the vein in his temple pulse as he visibly tensed and I thought for a second he was finally going to unleash all that pent-up rage on me.

"Ms. Kelly."

Startled, I looked up at a stout middle-aged woman who had just opened the office door across the hall from where Michael and I were waiting. She cleared her throat and pushed bright purple framed glasses up her broad face while casting a nervous glance towards Micheal.

"Yes?" I squeaked out, quickly hiding my hand back in the pocket of my jacket. I didn't dare look over at Michael, but could feel his satisfied smirk burning a hole in my head.

"They're ready for you now, ma'am."

I sighed and stood, casting one last glance down to my lucky shoes, and then touched the Saint Micheal pendant that always hung around my neck, sending up a silent prayer to the patron saint of law enforcement. If I'd had a four-leaf clover or rabbit's foot, I'd probably have touched those too, but so far Saint Michael and Louboutin had never failed me. I was counting on that now. Then I followed the secretary through the door, leaving Micheal, the not a saint one, to wait for me in the lobby.

When I entered the conference room, the secretary had ushered me toward; I felt my nerves settle like a ball of lead in my gut. David sat on one side of the large table next to two other people, one man and one woman. I scanned his face, trying to pick up on any subtle cues or hints he may give me about how the hearing had gone, but his face was impassive.

Directly to David's left sat a man I'd hoped to never have to meet. Assistant Director of the Office of Professional Responsibility, or OPR, Frank Reed was a thin man with a slightly receding hairline of light brown hair. His office was directly in charge of internal investigations of FBI agents and field offices. I was slightly surprised to see him in the seat next to David, though, or even in this office. Normally, the OPR sent their own investigators to dig up the dirt on agents under suspicion of misconduct. I swallowed past the lump in my throat. Maybe my charms had finally worn out their luck.

To Assistant Director Reed's left was a stern-looking blonde woman I'd only see glimpses of in hiring announcements or news bulletins. Angela Waters, Executive Assistant Director of the intelligence branch of the FBI. I could understand why Agent Reed was here, but to have the Executive Assistant for all of FBI Intelligence in the room overseeing my reinstatement hearing baffled me.

I paused in front of the table and tried to present myself as the professional and dedicated special agent that I was. Because ultimately it didn't matter why they were in this room, I had one goal today and that was to unravel the fucking mess my sister had made of my life.

"Senior Special Agent Hannah Kelly, thank you for joining us." Agent Reed began first and motioned for me to take the chair directly across from him.

"Thank you for having me sir," I looked from him to Agent Waters, "Ma'am."

My Memaw used to say, "You can't make a silk purse out of a sow's ear." Which basically meant you shouldn't expect to get something from nothing. She also used to say that about her neighbor Mrs. Billings, who she was always feuding with, but I think it meant something entirely different then. For now, though, I used the phrase to mean that if I wanted this meeting to go in the direction I needed it to, I would have to be on my best behavior. And maybe lay on the southern charm just a little thick.

Reed cleared his throat and tapped the thick manila envelope on the table in front of him. "Agent Kelly, I don't think I need to tell you how serious these accusations are against you. But after some serious discussion with Agent Williams and the evidence you brought forward, along with the sworn statements of your friends, I have decided that there can only be two outcomes to this hearing."

"They aren't my friends." The words were out of my mouth before I could blink and instantly winced in regret, especially when I saw Agent Waters arch one manicured eyebrow in intrigue.

"Pardon?" Agent Reed didn't look amused and cleared his throat again. I was beginning to wonder if it was a tick he had or if he genuinely needed a cough drop.

"I just mean that Ethan and Micheal aren't my friends." Rue's history with the bureau made me careful not to mention her. "I wouldn't even consider them colleagues. And while I appreciate they wrote statements verifying my account and Sybil's involvement in framing me, I do not feel that I owe them any debt of friendship, or that they reciprocate it." A brief tug of sadness whispered through me. At one point, I had begun to consider them friends. But now? I couldn't trust them and if there was one lesson, my sister had taught me over and over, was to not trust the people who were supposed to be there for you.

He cleared his throat again, and now I was sure it was some nervous tick, as he leaned back in his chair and looked first to Agent Waters and then to David. I wasn't sure what the silent exchange conveyed, but I suspected that it was confirming a conversation I hadn't been privy to.

"And yet you've agreed to continue to work with them in order to locate their missing team leader." This time it was the husky voice of Agent Waters that I turned towards. Her stony gaze studied me intensely. I had the eery feeling that I was being examined from the inside out. It was like the way Simon had analyzed me. As if he could read every thought. Only with Simon, I found myself wanting to open up to him. To show him every dark corner and secret thing I'd hidden away. Agent Waters, on the other hand, had me running to all my dirty closet doors and slamming them firmly shut. Somehow, I didn't think it would help, though.

"No ma'am. I did not agree to work with them to find Mr. Gallagher." I expected her to object to my statement, but she didn't flinch or speak, just waited for me to continue. "I couldn't give two shits what happens to Simon. I agreed to help them, and to ask your permission to do so, in order to find Sybil and bring her back to answer for her crimes."

Reed cleared his throat again, and I wondered how rude it would be if I offered him a cough drop from my purse. "You ask our permission now, but you didn't think to ask our permission when you went gallivanting off to Stockholm while you were under criminal investigation from the O.P.R.?"

I resisted the urge to squirm in my seat under the intense scrutiny of my three superiors across from me. That had probably been the hardest and most difficult conversation I'd ever had with David. When I'd gotten back from Stockholm and had filled him in on everything that happened, he'd looked at me with such disappointment that it felt like I was a kid getting scolded by my dad again.

"Hannah, how could you do something so stupid?"

"David, I didn't have a choice."

"Wrong, Hannah, there is always a choice. Always."

"I understand that what I did was and could be considered a conflict of interest. But I assure you, I had no intentions of violating the trust of my superiors or my government. Grief blinded me and made some poor decisions based on limited information." I swallowed and raised my chin a notch. Trusting the word of a Ghost and not going directly to my superior, David, with the information I had was foolish. But like everything that involved Sybil, I rushed headlong into the danger before even thinking about how it would affect me. White-hot rage flared through me. Even then, when she was supposed to have been dead, she'd been manipulating me. Controlling me. But it was still my decision to run off on a half-cocked mission without the bureau's stamp of approval. The blame could only fall squarely at my feet.

"And I am prepared to face the consequences of those decisions. I only ask that you allow me to rectify what I can and to retrieve the stolen evidence in the Hildago case. My sister needs to face justice in the U.S. I held my breath, meeting the cold gazes of the three people who were going to decide my fate. I could only see this going one of three ways. Either they reinstated me as an agent and let me go back to my job, they fired me and they would charge me with criminal conflict of interest, or they gave me a reprieve to hunt Sybil like I wanted. But Agent Reed had said he could only see two outcomes from this meeting, a criminaland now I wasn't so sure I knew my future after all.

CHAPTER THREE

Simon

I had no concept of time. No idea if it was day or night, morning or afternoon. I only knew the four walls that surrounded me. I didn't even have room to reach out and stretch my arms or sit in any comfortable position on the cold concrete. All I knew was that a thin slot in the door in front of me would open and blinding light would sting my eyes for a moment before a face would appear. Sometimes it was the scarred face of my jailer, someone I'd dubbed Mr. Ugly. Those were the good days. Sometimes it was Sybil's face. Those were the bad days.

Not because of any particular torture method she used on me. Oh no, Mr. Ugly had that pleasure. No, it was because sometimes when I looked at her, I couldn't help but see Hannah, and a deep regret would take hold of me.

I'd betrayed her intentionally, and I'd justified it because it was my job. My mission. My revenge. But as the days slipped on, I couldn't help but question my decisions.

I'd felt like I had no choice. Sybil was evil. She'd infiltrated my team and dug her poisonous claws into the woman I'd been in love with. In the end, it had forced me to do the unthinkable to protect the rest of my team. Evan, Rue, and Micheal would have all been sacrificed to feed Victoria's greed.

I'd then spent the last three years working to infiltrate their organization so that I could destroy it from the inside out.

But somehow, Sybil had managed to figure it out. She knew my game, knew my plan. And I had fallen right into her trap. But the one thing she hadn't counted on, the one thing I'd outsmarted her on, was Hannah.

The click of a metallic latch was the only warning I got just seconds before the tiny window slid open. A bright light pierced the darkness and caused my eyes to water in pain. I cracked a defiant grin, splitting the most recent cut on my lips wide. "Ah, Mr. Ugly. So nice to see you today, sir. Did ye bring me that Scotch I told you about?"

Dull brown eyes glared at me, but instead of responding, the small window was slammed closed again. I wanted to cry out as the panic rose. *"No! Don't leave me here in the dark again!"* But just as I was about the give into the temptation the door swung open and all seven feet of burly Russian muscle, his semi-automatic rifle pointed directly at my face, stood before me. I sighed with relief. Strange that his beatings were preferable to the dark, but that's how torture worked.

Advanced S.E.R.E. schools had done their job in training for these moments. It was inevitable in the life of a government asset that, at some point, the enemy would attempt to extract information by whatever means they felt necessary. Most typically, it was torture if sex or bribery didn't work. And since Sybil had quickly realized that she didn't hold the same sway over my libido that Hannah did, or that threats of giving me over to certain terrorist organizations didn't bother me, they'd resorted to good old-fashioned torture and beatings.

And that was something that I could handle, but even the strongest man would break after untold hours left in the dark. So I happily left my cell, naked and bloodied, to proceed in front of my silent partner in this nightmare for another round of what I'd begun to dub sessions.

I played a game with my Russian jailer, although I doubted he would ever realize it. In this game, I would talk to him, even through the blood that I'd choke back. My S.E.R.E. instructors probably wouldn't appreciate this method. But after days and hours of repeating the same patterns; name, birth-date, I'm a citizen of the United Kingdom and I'd like to speak to my ambassador. I'd finally broke.

Now, I talked to Mr. Ugly as if we were old chums meeting up for a pint at the local pub. I talked incessantly about any and every little thing I could think of. Honestly, I was at the point where I was running out of things I could tell him. But another thing they emphasized in all these advanced undercover units was to make yourself as human as possible, and so I did.

"Do you have the time?" I asked as he pressed the cold steel of his gun into my back, indicating that I should step into the elevator doors that opened in front of us. He didn't answer, of course, just shoved me harder forward and I stumbled inside.

"Don't get yer knickers twisted there, mate. Just making conversation. You know, I feel like our relationship has been a bit one-sided lately. I've got the perfect game to fix it. Ever heard of twenty questions?"

The only response I got was a grunt and the

blinding pain of his gun slamming into my ribs. Coughing, I slid against the side of the elevator and grinned. "Och, come on, mate. You have to get bored with using me as a punching bag. I mean, I'm flattered, but I can't be your only hobby, right?"

He didn't answer and stared at me with those dead eyes while continuing to train his gun on me. I pushed away from the wall as the elevator sank slowly down to the depths of the hell that was waiting for me.

"Ok, maybe you need a lesson in how the game works. I ask twenty questions to get to know ye and then you get twenty questions to get to know me. Ready? Ok, I'll go first. Do you like Madonna?"

Brown eyes blinked slowly, and I nodded. "Ok, I'm taking that as a yes. You know, I'm a bit fond of her me-self. Ye strike me as the Material Girl era fan, though."

He raised his lip in a snarl and took a step toward me.

"Whoa there, big guy. Got it. Yer not a Madonna fan. Spice Girls maybe? Who's your favorite? Personally, I've always had a thing for Posh..."

Suddenly the elevator came to a stop, and the doors slid open with a soft swoosh revealing a flushed-looking Sybil Kelley on the other side.

"What took you so long?" Her voice was strained,

her skin pale as she took in my naked state. "Get him to the loading dock. Now, we have to leave."

Mr. Ugly grabbed me as panic rose again. They were moving me, but I didn't understand why. "Wait, where are you-..." Pain exploded through my head as the butt of Mr. Ugly's gun came down on it and I fell down to my knees. Blinking away the fuzziness, I groaned as I was grabbed and hauled back to my feet, then half dragged towards an open warehouse door.

It was then that I noticed that there was movement all around us. People in black uniforms were moving and loading boxes and crates into large moving vehicles. Electronics were being packed and unplugged furiously as Sybil screamed orders at people in white lab coats. Understanding dawned and I couldn't help the chuckle that escaped me. Sybil's head whipped around towards me and I grinned, half leaning against my Russian captor.

"What do you find so amusing, Mr. Gallagher?" Her voice was sharp, a snarl curling at her lip.

"They're coming, aren't they?" I grinned like an idiot, loving the sight of the pristine Sybil Kelly devolving into a paranoid panic in front of me.

"I have no clue what or whom you're referring to, Mr. Gallagher." One brow arched in that familiar haughty way I was used to seeing by now. The one that said she knew I was lying through my teeth even as she continued to torture me. The one that said she didn't care when I passed out from the pain of it.

"Tsk... yes you do. My team found me, didn't they? And they're on the way right now to mess up yer pretty little operation." If my team was indeed on the way, I needed to stall as long as I could so that they could get here before everything was moved or destroyed. We needed the evidence that was being carried away.

She stalked towards me, every inch of her vibrating in rage. "So, this is why you've been so resistant to my efforts. Have you been holding out hope this whole time? Did you think that if you could just outlast our little sessions, you'd survive long enough for your team to track you down?"

I swallowed as her words sunk into me. Yes, that's exactly what I'd thought. But as I watched people scurrying like roaches from the light, I worried we were too late. "Well, if it's not my team coming for me, then why are you running away like a scared little girl?"

"I'm not running, Mr. Gallagher. I'm preparing. There's a distinct difference." She cocked her head and gave me an appraising look, then grinned. "You truly don't know, do you?"

"Know that yer a psychotic, sadistic bitch? Oh, I'm well aware of that, Dr. Kelly."

She tipped her head back and laughed. The sound startled everyone and for a moment all the frenzied movement stopped. "Oh, Simon. I thought my sister was an idiot, but you just might surpass her for the first place prize. You two would actually be perfect for each other."

She waved her arm in a sweep around the warehouse, and movement began again. "You've been trying to outsmart me for three years now and look at where it's gotten you. Your lover is dead, your team is disbanded, and you walked the one person I want to destroy the most in the world right into my web."

A sickening feeling clawed at my gut, which I'd never hoped to feel or experience again.

She took another step towards me and leaned up until her lips were brushing against my ear. "No, Simon, do not mistake this for fear. This is *anticipation*. Because the minute Hannah tries to come for me, I will have her *exactly* where I want her. And then I'm going to kill her."

....

CHAPTER FOUR

....

Hannah

"Line was bloody long, and I didn't know whatever fancy mood mover you preferred, so I just ordered the one that looked like it had the most chocolate." Evan placed a thick-handled mug of coffee in front of me before pulling out the chair to my left and sitting down. To anyone in the small bookstore and coffee shop, we were a pair of tourists taking in a popular Instagram photo spot in the capital of Turkey, Ankara.

Soon after my reinstatement hearing, I'd once again found myself packed up and on an overseas flight to a new country I'd never expected to visit. We'd gotten word through some of Evan's connections that Sergei had been spotted here in Ankara making deals with some corrupt government officials. Micheal and Rue had gone ahead of us to do some recon and establish our safe house. Now Evan and I were following up on a lead, that Sergei had a friend in the same area as this coffee shop. A Russian antique dealer who owned the store across the street.

Picking up my mug, I sniffed at the steam coming up from the lid. "What made you think I'd prefer the one with the most chocolate?" Cold blue eyes twinkled with slight amusement and a dimple flashed behind the brim of his cup. "I make it my business to know."

I took a sip but resisted the urge to sigh with delight as the dark chocolate mocha did its magic. I didn't want to give into his ego any more than I needed to. It was over-inflated enough already. "That line might work with some other women, E, but I know you don't actually care about what kind of coffee I like to drink." I took another sip and decided that coffee in the states would never taste the same or as good again.

"You're right. I didn't notice what kind of coffee you liked, or that you have a chocolate addiction, but Simon did."

I angled my head towards him and glared. "I believe Simon knew my coffee preferences even less than I believe you actually pay attention to a woman you don't intend to fuck." Evan's easygoing manner turned frosty and the playboy smile disappeared in a flash. Suddenly I was staring at the face that greeted me all those weeks ago in the Atlanta safe house and somehow I knew that I'd really been interacting with this Evan all along. The dimples, the jokes, and the carefree attitude were nothing but a mask for the cold, merciless killer that lie beneath it.

"Trust me when I tell you I notice more than you think, Hannah Kelly. And I promise you don't want to be on the receiving end of my attentions." He leaned in closer and I could smell the crisp scent of his after-shave. Something that reminded me of the bite of bitter cold and frost. The hair on the back of my neck stood on end and I shivered despite the warm coffee. Or maybe I'd been up too late reading one of my favorite fantasy novels.

I stared at him for what seemed like an eternity, wondering how seriously I should take his threat while simultaneously calculating all the ways he could hide my body before he tipped his head back and laughed so loud that several people in the area turned towards us. My cheeks flushed with embarrassment as I realized how easily he'd trolled me. "Jesus Christ, Evan, that wasn't funny." "Oi, but the look on your face was." He grinned, the psychopath mask displaced by an impish grin once more. The change in his persona was going to give me whiplash. "I wasn't sure if you were going to shoot me first, or run." He snickered and took a sip of his own coffee, throwing an arm across the back of my seat as if he owned it. I glanced down at where it draped before picking it up and placing it firmly back in his own space. What was with these alpha-hole men I'd surrounded myself with and their lack of respect for personal space? "One, I don't run. Two, I'm still thinking about shooting you." He arched a blonde brow and tipped his coffee towards me in a mock toast. "I would expect nothing less from the woman who managed to get Simon so twisted up he actually gave a damn about something other than the mission for once."

I turned away from his toast, uncomfortable at the direction our conversation had turned. I didn't want to think about Simon or how twisted he was over me. It was bad enough that I couldn't deny that I was just as twisted up over him. Only the pit in my stomach had nothing to do with feelings and everything to do with what Agent Reed had said to me before I left the conference room the day of my hearing.

His departing words echoed in my mind. *"You have one mission here, Agent Kelly. Just do your job."* Or lose your *job, and more.* He hadn't needed to say those words out loud. The threat had been read and understood loud and clear.

The coffee turned bitter on my tongue and I pushed it from before glancing up to the shop across the street from us. Our stakeout location couldn't have been more picture-perfect and I could see why so many bloggers were interested in it. We were seated in a covered patio area that butted up to the sidewalk and gave us an unobstructed view of the street and shops that lined it. The patio was semi-enclosed with a red painted lattice on two sides and a half-wall that faced the street painted the same deep red. There were lush vines and plants scaling its sides, making it both cozy and dark. We could see all the comings and goings of the pedestrians visiting the shops, but anyone on the street would have to step directly up to the patio and look inside to know who was watching them.

Hiding my discomfort, I fiddled with my phone and pretended to take a few photos of my mug against the backdrop of the creeping vines. "I think you may have me confused with someone else. Simon made it very obvious that he lets nothing, especially a woman, get in the way of his objective."

Evan took my phone from me with a slight frown and held it up so the camera was facing me. "Hannah, seriously? Where have you been carrying this thing?" He then proceeded to take out a soft cloth from the inner pocket of his jacket and started wiping the lens free of fingerprints and smudges. "And you're wrong. Before you, Simon was hell-bent on doing whatever it took to get to Sybil."

I snorted and snatched my phone back from him. "I can't tell if you all are just pathological liars or delusional. You do remember that Simon tricked me into coming to Stockholm with you maniacs just to get my sister to come out of hiding, right? He literally used me to get to her."

Evan shook his head and sighed. "You're right, partly." Evan leaned into me, his hand covering mine and stopping my half-hearted photography attempts. "Hannah, you have no idea what Simon, what *we* went through to get to Sybil and take down Sergei. For the past three years now, we've been trying to infiltrate their organization and, for once, we were so close. We almost had her. But Sybil has always seemed to be just one step ahead."

He released my hand and sat back, turning towards the street, his gaze darkening in frustration. "It was like she had no weaknesses. Nothing that we could use to exploit or get some sort of leverage on her." Blue eyes swiveled back to me. "Until you."

"What do you mean?" I was no longer paying attention to the people around me or the shop we were supposed to be monitoring. "Sybil hid everything from me. I was completely in the dark about her life. Everything she told me, ever, has been a massive fucking lie."

He nodded. "And that's why you became the key to her undoing. When Si realized that you truly didn't know about Sybil's secret life, he did some more digging, and that's when he discovered her hatred and obsession with you. He knew that if he made you the bait in his trap, she wouldn't be able to resist. And he was right."

I curled my hands into fists in my lap, anger coursing through me again. "You aren't exactly building a case for your friend. I was just an asset to be used, in his opinion."

"Yeah, at first you were. You were just an asset to all of us. But something changed and I can't tell you what exactly it was or when. But I can tell you one thing, until you, Simon Gallagher, would never have let Sybil or Sergei walk away from that ballroom that night alive. And if he didn't care about you, he wouldn't have let you walk away either."

I swallowed, remembering how Simon had stood there, silent and stoic, while I'd aimed my gun at him. The gun he'd given to me right before we'd left for the gala.

"Why?" I whispered. "Why does Simon hate my sister so much?"

Evan didn't speak for a moment, just stared into the

inky black of the coffee in the mug in front of him. Then, when he did, his words came out in a whisper. The darkness in his voice betraying his emotions. Evan was just as affected by whatever had happened as Simon was. "Because she forced him to kill the woman he loved. Victoria. My sister."

CHAPTER FIVE

Hannah

It felt like the wind had been knocked out of me at Evan's revelation. But just as I was about to ask him to explain further, his head shot up and his gaze laser focused onto the little shop across the street from us.

"He's on the move. Let's go."

We abandoned our coffees and exited the patio through a little side gate that connected to the street. Pedestrian traffic flowed around us as people stopped at little stalls filled with trinkets, jewelry, and brightly colored pottery wares. A few yards ahead, I could see Sergei's figure, at least a full head taller than most of the shoppers, winding his way through the crowd.

Evan's voice spoke low into his jacket lapel. "Move to intercept on my word."

Michael's rich voice filled the little mic inserted into my ear. "Roger, moving into position."

We wove in and out of the flow of people, the scents and noises of the ancient city a muted backdrop to the sound of my heart beating in my ears. Any other time, I would have been awestruck at the beauty that surrounded me. But as it was, I barely registered that I was walking the same cobbled streets that birthed the ancient Ottoman empire. All I could see was Sergei's silver head bobbing ahead, and I had to fight the urge to surge forward and tackle him to the ground.

We would only get this one chance to grab him and if he somehow managed to escape, then all chances of finding Sybil or Simon were gone. Anxiousness made my steps speed up, trying to not let him out of my sight until I felt a hand on my arm jolting me to stop. I turned to glare at Evan, but he signaled to follow before ducking into a small shop, and with a quick glance at Sergei's retreating figure, I followed after him.

The shop was dimly lit and smelled like a mix of spices and incense. Clay pots, brass pitchers turned green with age, and colorful fabrics were stacked in haphazard piles on a few tables, spilling onto the floor. Scarves and beads lined the walls in shades of rusted red and blue turquoise. Evan gave a quick nod to the owner, who seemed to be dozing against a stack of what looked like oriental rugs, and had barely lifted his head to glance in our direction.

Then we were winding our way through the piles of goods and random items towards a door in the back. Evan paused, peering through the slats into a dimly lit and narrow back alley.

"Evan..." I growled with impatience. But he just held his hand up to silence me once more and continue to watch the alley. Finally, after what seemed like forever, he turned and held up three fingers. Eyes widening with understanding, I pulled my weapon from the holster tucked secretly against my ribs and flicked the safety off. Evan did the same, and we stayed there against the door, staring at each other for a long heart-beat before he quietly mouthed. "One, two, three..." And then he burst through the door into the alley and turned to his left, coming face to face with our target.

I followed close to his back as he took point, doing a quick sweep of the alleyway behind us and looking up to scan the rooftops of the buildings that rose on either side. Part of me didn't believe that it could be this simple, or easy, but when I finally looked at Sergei and saw the fury blazing in his cold gaze, I realized he was so arrogant he hadn't considered that anybody would come after him.

I moved forward and stepped in front of Evan,

letting him guard my back, my weapon never leaving Sergei's large frame.

"Hey Serg... can I call you Serg? Long time no see. How's my bitch sister doing? Still got your balls in a chokehold?"

Recognition replaced fury when he saw me, and one corner of his lip curled in a snarl. "You are as pathetic as your sister said you were."

"Oof... I'll take that as a yes, then." I flicked my gun up and down his frame. "Only it looks like this pathetic sister has a bit of the upper hand at the moment, doesn't it?"

His fists clenched at his sides, and I could see the large vein across his forehead bulge. I grinned,"Sissy, ever tell you about our Memaw?" I didn't wait for him to answer and continued on, "Memaw was a bit of a character, always had these crazy sayings she was muttering under breath. Everyone thought she had a few screws loose upstairs, but I loved her to pieces. See, in the south we feel a certain way about the crazy in our families. We don't shy away from it. Nope, we prop it upright on the front porch and show it off to the neighbors." I shook my head and smiled sadly at the memory of my grandmother. "Do you know what Memaw always said about Sybil? A little powder, a little paint, makes a girl look what she ain't."

I took a step forward and could feel the fury radiating off of him in waves. "It's an old southern expression that means that no matter what you do to dress it up, you can't fix ugly." Pain gripped my heart, and I had to fight not to let the deep hurt and betrayal make my voice shake. "I didn't know it then, but Memaw was telling me exactly the kind of ugly that Sybil hid inside.

"Do you think by telling me this that somehow you're going to earn my sympathy?" Sergei scoffed. "Do you think I'll suddenly flip for you? All this does is confirm everything Sybil has said. You are a jealous fool who did nothing but hold her back from achieving her dreams."

Rage flared, and I took another step forward, ignoring Evan's low warning voice behind me. I was standing mere inches from him now, his larger frame casting a shadow over me. "Sybil was my life. I gave up everything *for* her. Even my memories. I hid everything down deep and forgot all the times she tortured me just to get what she wanted. Like being born was a mistake, and she was determined to right the wrong."

"Because you are a mistake." Sergei hissed and leaned down, not caring that the barrel of my gun was practically pressed against his sternum. At any moment, I could pull the trigger and a dark part of me whispered to just do it. Hadn't I seen how evil this man was? How much damage he had done? One bullet could end it and then maybe, finally, Sybil would know that I wasn't

afraid of her anymore. For once, I'd be the one getting what I wanted.

I seethed with rage as Sergei's cold blue gaze bore into mine, daring me to do it. Then, with a smug smile, as if he saw in my gaze exactly what he was looking for, pulled back. "For a moment, I thought you might prove your sister wrong. That you might actually have the, what's the American phrase you use? Balls? To pull the trigger. But my moya lyubov' is right as always. You have been a thorn in her side for far too long. A dark obsession that has prevented her from focusing on our mission and goals. It will be a pleasure to deliver you to her."

I cocked my head, confused by his words. "Deliver me? What kind of psycho nonsense are you monologing about, Serg?" Just then a crackle came through the mic in my ear and Rue's voice filled the void in-between the static. "We need to hurry this up. I've got two vehicles fast approaching from the west. They will intercept your location in less than two minutes."

Fuck. Figured Sergei wouldn't let himself be exposed for too long. Or perhaps the Turkish government had figured out we weren't exactly here on a desert pleasure cruise. Evan closed in behind me just as Micheal peeled away from the thick shadows of the alley walls like he'd been born there. Considering the dark glint in his black eyes, my assumption wasn't too far off. "Ok well, this has been a great get to know you, but I'm afraid we don't have time for southern goodbyes."

Sergei grinned and crossed his arms. "Did you think you were the only one with connections in Ankara? I have been here waiting for you and your little band of misfits. You are playing a game you do not understand. A game you will most certainly lose."

I snorted and just grinned. "Yeah, now I'm sure Sybil didn't tell you about our Memaw."

Sergei frowned. "Sybil's family is of no consequences to me."

"Yeah, well, if she'd have told you about Memaw you might have learned a thing or two."

"Such as?"

"Such as that Memaw was the queen of cards at her little old ladies' church club." I grinned as Micheal continued his stealthy death slide towards Sergei. "She won every game." Swift as jungle cat Micheal struck, and the needle containing enough sedative to dose a gorilla sank deep into his neck. Sergei dropped like a sack of potatoes to the dirt packed ground and I followed him down, enjoying the anger and surprise that flashed, then quickly faded as he began to slip away, unconscious. "And she liked to cheat."

CHAPTER SIX

Simon

The cold metal bench I was sitting on felt like it was going to be permanently molded to my backside by the time we reached wherever it was that we were going. I shifted, trying to relieve the numbness that was creeping down into my thighs and cast a glance to the doors in the back of the van, hoping that the next time it came to a stop for a guard change I might get a glimpse of the scenery and be able to determine our location. Stretching my legs out as much as possible in the cramped space, I clenched and unclenched my thighs, willing blood flow back into them. One of the current duo of guards glared and kicked my foot before saying in a thick Russian accent and broken English, "Move, foot."

Other than a brief stop to relieve myself after I'd threatened to piss on the previous guard shift, I hadn't been allowed out of the van even to stretch my legs. Even then, they'd placed a bag over my head and other than the knowledge that I was on some sort of dirt road, I'd had no sense of location or direction. At least I was no longer naked. Not that the grey jumpsuit Mr. Ugly had forced me into offered much in the way of extra padding.

The guard kicked my foot again, and I snarled in response. I was tired, ass-numb, and starving. In short, I was itching for a fight and anything to break up the monotony of the forced road trip. At this point, I would have almost preferred the dark solitude of my cell. At least then I knew I'd be getting a proper meal. The guard shifted forward, sensing a rising threat in his mostly docile prisoner. I smirked, a little bit of the icy darkness I'd kept a lid on creeping into my gaze, and stretched my legs out further until my bare foot and his booted one and we were practically playing footsie with each other.

It was a risk to taunt my captors this way, and not one my survival instructors would have advised me to take. But I was done playing the good little prisoner. I had no clue what was happening in the outside world and for all I knew I had compromised my team, burned as they called it in the espionage world, and were on the run. Or worse.

I pushed down the fear that threatened to rise, refusing to believe that Micheal, Rue and Evan were in danger because of me. Because of the choices I'd made. I only hoped that if they were burned, they'd managed to get Hannah to safety first. Whatever guilt I felt for the poor choices I'd made when it came to my team paled in comparison to what I felt over Hannah.

She'd been innocent. Innocent and still guilty by association, in my mind. Even after I'd realized how little she had to do with Sybil's twisted games, and that she was just as much a victim, if not more, than the rest of us, I'd still gone through with the plan. I'd still convinced my team it was the right thing to do. All I wanted, all I cared about, was the mission objective. All I could see was my revenge.

My guard leaned across the cramped space, his hot breath washing over my face, "Move. Your. Foot." and then he brought the barrel of his automatic weapon up until it was nearly touching my chest. I leaned forward to close the gap and smiled.

"Make me." And then I exploded, bringing my hand cuffed arms up, wrapping the short length of chain around the barrel of his gun so fast he didn't have time to register before it was pulled from his grasp. At the same time, I hooked my leg behind his, trapping him from moving, as I gained control of the weapon and slammed the butt directly into his face. Blood spurted as his nose was shattered and he slumped back unconscious. Meanwhile, his partner who had been dosing next to him woke with a start and began shouting in Russian as he lunged for me. The van came to a screeching halt and jerked us forward so that we ended up crashing into each other and by some gods forsaken miracle, no bullets started flying as both our weapons were flung away from us.

The guard landed on top of me and I grunted at his weight and the pain that burst through my ribs, the results of my sessions with Mr. Ugly. But at this point, I didn't care. My time with them was coming to an end, whether or not they wanted it to. The guard sat up, allowing me the room I needed to grab his arm and yank it down across my body, then trapped one of his legs with mine as I thrust my hips up and flipped him, reversing our positions. He struggled, attempting to land blows, when he realized I had the upper hand now. I pressed the weight of my forearm into his neck, slowly cutting off the blood supply to his brain.

Just then, the doors to the back of the van were flung open and bright sunlight illuminated the dim cargo space. I had barely enough time to scramble backwards, while maneuvering the unconscious guard so that he was now a shield for the half dozen automatic weapons that were aimed at me. I squinted into the blinding light, barely able to make out the shapes of the militant men in-front of me. And then a smaller figure stepped forward and gave me an appraising look.

"I wondered when your poor tortured prisoner act would drop and the real Simon would make himself known." Sybil's cold voice sent chills down my spine. I had expected her to be on a flight somewhere half-way across the world, not escorting me to wherever their new base was.

"Slumming it with the hired guns now, Sybil? I thought that was beneath you."

She smiled, just a small sinister twist of her lips. "No Simon, it was beneath Tory. Or did you forget how she told you she was done playing in the mud and dirt with you?"

She was taunting me, purposely bringing up my dead lover's name to throw me off guard. I shook my head. "Nah, that's the bullshit you fed her, Sybil. But I'm not discussing the past with you anymore. You're going to tell your little friends to step back and drop their weapons, and then you're going to let me walk out of here."

She cocked her head and glanced at the guard slumped against the wall of the van, blood covering his face, and then the one who was starting to come around in my arms, even as my hands gripped his head and neck, ready to snap it in a moments notice. "Or what? You'll kill them?" She grinned then and the next thing a knew had a gun raised and two shots were fired off in quick succession.

The man in my arms went limp again, dead. I didn't need to look over at the other guard to know he wouldn't be waking up either. I glared at Sybil and the pistol she was aiming at my head.

"Now, are you going to sit back and be a good boy, Simon? Or do I need to remind you, again, that I am the one in control here?"

I slowly raised my hands up, the guards body falling with a thud to the blood slicked van floor and placed them on my head. Never taking my eyes off of Sybil's, letting the rage and hatred I felt burn through them.

"Why are you keeping me alive, Sybil?" I stayed perfectly still as her other men climbed into the van beside me and began pulling out the bodies of their comrades. If they felt remorse or grief over their deaths, they didn't show it. She shrugged, a casual movement that didn't seem natural to her. "Perhaps it's for my own amusement. Perhaps I do it for Tory's memory. After all, I don't think she would have enjoyed your death as much as you enjoyed hers."

She was taunting me again.

"No, you don't care about sentiments. Even sick ones like that. You're keeping me alive for a reason."

"Please don't let your inflated ego read more into this situation than what it is. You're my prisoner, my pawn, and right now you're more valuable to me alive than dead."

"Valuable as what? You know you're not going to get any information out of me. No government will claim knowledge of me. And the longer you keep me alive, the longer you risk my team finding me." For a moment I saw the mask that Sybil kept in place slip, pure rage burning through her eyes.

"I do not need to explain myself to you, Simon. I am not Tory, begging for your pathetic permission. Or Hannah, easily manipulated into following where you go on some self-righteous mission. I'll keep you a live as long as I need to and then you will die when you are no longer useful to me."

Sybil stepped back from the van as two more guards grabbed my arms and hauled me to my feet, dragging me into the bright sunlight. I was able to get a good look at my surrounds for the first time and realized we were in a small clearing. Tall trees on either side of us were beginning to turn bright shades of orange and red, as fall was descending on the European countryside. What country it was I couldn't be sure, especially since for a good portion of my captivity I had been unconscious, but based of the geography I was sure we were in Eastern Europe, close to the Russian border.

I took the brief reprieve from the cramped van to take stock of my situation. Other than the one I'd just exited, there were two other matching vans parked away from us, blocking the seemingly only entrance into the clearing. The forest surrounding us was thick and dark despite the midday sun. I turned in a slow circle before looking at Sybil once more and grinned.

"Ye know, Sybil, for as smart as ye are, you have a thing or two to learn still about tactics. Maybe ye should stick to academics and let yer boyfriend do the nasty business of torture and weapons dealing."

She'd been speaking in a low voice to one of her men, but whirled and glared at me. For some reason, the cold and calculating scientist was unnerved, and I had a sickening suspicion why.

"I did not ask your opinion, nor is it necessary, Mr. Gallagher."

I ignored her and motioned with my head toward the clearing entrance. "For example, ye've nearly boxed yerself in there. Almost like yer setting up a defensive position, but ye picked a poor place. Not only are ye boxed in, ye don't have an escape route."

She smirked, "Do you really want to know why I kept you alive, Simon?"

Her question threw me off, thinking we'd already

dropped the subject. "Please," I bowed my head towards her as if I wasn't standing in a clearing surrounded by armed guards, shackled, beaten, and covered in blood that wasn't my own. "... enlighten me."

"Gladly." She drawled, just a hint of the southern accent Hannah had in her voice. "Because of her." She nodded into the distance over my shoulder and I frowned, genuinely confused, but turned to follow the direction of her gaze and suddenly my entire world narrowed down into one singular moment as I watched a brown-haired vixen in a black leather jacket hopped out from the driver's side of a blacked out SUV and look, not at me, but her sister.

"I told you, Simon," Sybil's voice slithered into my ear. "You walked her right into my web and now I'm going to kill her."

CHAPTER SEVEN

Hannah

I opened the SUV's door and was met with the cool and crisp early autumn air of the western border of Estonia. We were close to the Russian border, and it wasn't my first pick of meeting places, but it was the one thing Sybil wouldn't budge on. Either we met here, or we didn't meet at all. I could have pushed my luck, but that would have meant I revealed my cards too early, and if Memaw taught me anything, it was to know when to hold em' and when to fold em'.

Three identical vans were in the clearing with us, one of them moving to close in behind our vehicle and block the narrow entrance to the clearing. We were now trapped and between me and Sybil, there stood at least a dozen armed mercenaries and only god knows what else. I didn't trust that she didn't have some of her own merchandise on hand to use in sticky situations like this, or that bringing me out to the middle of nowhere Eastern Europe wasn't also an effective way to kill two birds with one stone. Me and Simon. Speaking of, my heart lurched when I spared the barest glance in his direction.

He looked like shit on a stick, and that was putting it nicely. Sharp cheekbones were exaggerated from weeks of maltreatment and torture. Dark stubble covered his face and his normally carefully coifed hair was a matted mess of darkness. The jumpsuit he wore was stained with what looked like blood or worse and I swallowed thickly, silently praying that it wasn't his.

Ever since the conversation with Evan back at the Turkish coffee shop, I'd been going over the night at the gala in my head. Simon making sure I had a weapon at the last minute. Simon disappearing and telling me to hide near the dance floor. Simon standing there, never saying a word in his defense while Sybil had ranted and raved at me, and I'd had that same gun aimed at his head. Simon saving me and dragging me out of the building as they raided it. Simon slamming the van door shut and watching me disappear into the night. Into safety.

Sybil was the first to speak, and she took a couple

of steps toward me.

"Well, you actually came. Not that I'm surprised. You are a good little dog, after all. Much better than that awful puppy you kept."

Rage threatened to black out my vision but somehow I managed to keep my voice from shaking as I took a step towards her as well.

"I came because you have something that belongs to me, and I want it back."

Sybil turned to look at Simon before turning back to me. "You really came to get the man who lied to you, used you, and then left you for dead? Are you that desperate for someone to love Hannah?" A sardonic grin parted her lips. "So says the woman who went behind my back and ruined every relationship I've ever had. Are you so obsessed with me that you need to chase my sloppy seconds?" I grinned right back at her, thrilled to see anger contort her beautiful features as I finally revealed the chink in her armor.,"But no, I didn't come for Simon. I want the Hildago papers you stole from our evidence locker. Give them back."

I tried not to see how Simon flinched when I revealed I wasn't there for him. But I couldn't reveal any weaknesses to Sybil at this point. She was a shark and the minute she smelled blood in the water, she'd pounce. I needed her to be off her guard until the last possible minute, or we were all dead.

Anger was replaced by a flicker of surprise, and then she tipped her head back and laughed. "Really Hannah? You came all this way, put yourself in a ridiculous amount of danger, just to get evidence on some pathetic human trafficking ring?" Her laughter rang through the clearing and I shifted from one foot to the other, fingers flexing at my sides as I tried not to let her get to me. This was what she had done since we were children. Belittled my ideas, made me think I was stupid or crazy. I'd let her do it when we were younger, but no more.

"Yep." I let the P pop and crossed my arms, staring her down and daring her to say anything else. "And since Mom and Dad clearly didn't teach you that stealing isn't what good young ladies do, I'm going to have to do it instead. So here's how this is going to go. You're going to give me the evidence back. You're going to tell your little band of merry-men with machine guns to go take a hike. And then you're going to come back with me and answer for your crimes."

She was still smiling when I finished my last sentence and shook her head. "Hannah, you are such the gullible fool. You know it's actually been boring keeping you in the dark all these years? I kept hoping at some point you'd finally wake up and realize who it was that was sabotaging everything you ever did, but you were just so determined to think that I was your poor, sweet, innocent baby sister who needed you for protecting."

I felt her words like a stab in the heart. That's exactly how I'd seen her. My beautiful baby sister, the one person I wanted to protect from the world. Instead, I had to protect the world from her.

"Not going to argue with you there. It was pretty stupid of me not to see you for what you really are, Sybil." I cocked my head to the side and gave her a slow sweep of my gaze, cataloging every minor aspect of her. "A spoiled, selfish little girl who didn't learn how to share. And so long as we all gave in to want you wanted, you kept quiet. But the minute anyone stepped out of line, you'd throw a giant hissy fit. Mom and Dad should have whooped your tail. Honestly, I'm surprised they never did. But here we are, just dealing with another one of Sybil's bratty temper tantrums."

I thought for a moment that she was going to launch herself across the clearing at me, rage practically vibrating through her entire body. "You have no idea what our mother and father did to me. Maybe instead of hunting me down, you should have started asking questions from dear old Mom and dad."

"I didn't want to upset them anymore than they already are. They already had to go through your *murder*, Sybil. Why crush them anymore with the giant disappointment you turned out to be? Who wants to find out their kid is a psychopath?"

Her eyes narrowed, and she gave me a tight smile. "Indeed, who *would* want to find out their kid is a psychopath?" She crossed her arms over her chest and for a moment I saw a glimpse of the Sybil I remembered. Vulnerable, sad, and lost. I steeled my resolve and raised my chin. No matter what I remembered, I had to face the now. *This* Sybil was manipulative, conniving, and completely out for her own gain. I couldn't even be sure the little girl I remembered was real, or just a false memory my mind created to cover up the horrible things she'd done to me. Things I'd wanted to forget.

"Your time is up, Sybil. Hand over the documents and tell your men to leave."

She smiled. "Or what? You are far out of your league here, sister dear. You always were."

"You know it's funny sis, your boyfriend said the same thing."

Sybil stilled. "What do you mean?"

I shrugged casually. "Oh, just that when we talked, he had a very similar statement to make about me being out of my league. You know, for someone who claims to know you so well, doesn't seem like you've told him much about our family. He had no clue who Memaw was."

Sybil raised her gun and took a few more steps forward. Suddenly, the crisp autumn air turned even colder as tension and danger filled the atmosphere. All eyes and guns were trained on me. I thought I heard Simon growl a low warning, but he was standing too far away to hear and I couldn't afford to take my eyes off of Sybil.

"You're bluffing." She snarled at me and motioned for a few of her men to advance towards me.

"Tsk," I shook my head, "Now who's out of their league? First rule of hostage negotiations: never assume the person you're negotiating with is bluffing." At that moment, the back door to the SUV opened and Sergei's gigantic frame was dropped unceremoniously to the ground. He groaned and shuffled to his knees as best he could, considering his hands and feet were zip-tied. I couldn't help but grin at the audible gasp of shock that escaped Sybil's lips. Her eyes widened at the sight of her lover's bloody and bruised face. I'd been hesitant about leaving Sergei under Micheal's care while we were setting up the meeting with Sybil, but after seeing how well they'd treated Simon, I no longer had any regrets. Sergei deserved every bruise and broken bone he received. A pound of flesh, for a pound of flesh.

"Sergei!" She surged forward to get to him and then

jumped back as a bullet struck the ground mere inches from where he was kneeling. *Good job Evan.*

I moved closer to Sergei and placed a hand on his shoulder. "Here's how this is going to go, Sissy. I'll repeat it one more time since you didn't seem to understand the first time. You're going to give me the evidence you stole. You're going to tell your men to get the fuck away from here. You're going to come with me willingly." I patted Sergei's shoulder. "Oh! *And* you're going to let Simon go free. Or my friend that's sitting comfy cozy in his sniper nest about a mile from here will blow first Sergei's brains out, then yours, and you'll be food for the crows."

I watched as she stood there with her mouth gaped open, staring at where the bullet had struck the ground before looking back to stare at Sergei. Behind her, I could see Simon advancing slowly towards us while his captors were distracted, his gaze never leaving me. I frowned when I saw the dark glint in his gaze, but he kept his face an unreadable mask. Whatever he felt, he would not reveal it just yet. He only watched, advancing inch by inch, until he was mere feet from me.

Turning back to Sybil, I arched a brow. "Well? Time's ticking, sister. What's it going to be?"

Sybil turned towards me and snarled, "You bitch." And then she aimed her gun and fired.

CHAPTER EIGHT

Hannah

I felt the impact of the ground before I realized what had happened. All around us, people were shouting and the sound of automatic weapons and Evan's sniper rifle were echoing off the trees. Dust and the smell of gunpowder filled my nose. A heaviness weighed me down and I turned my head to see Simon's grey eyes, wild and raging as they stared into mine while he hovered over me.

"We have to move." He growled into my ear and I shivered at the sound, before rolling off of me with a grunt. I moved to follow him, but was stopped by a ricochet of bullets next to me. Scrambling as fast as I could, I reached into my boot and pulled out my gun before returning fire in the direction I thought the shots were coming from.

"Hannah! Simon!" Michael's voice rang out over the sound of bullets flying and then I heard Rue in my ear. "Evan and Michael are providing cover fire. Get Simon and get to the vehicle. You need to get out of there."

Just then I looked up to see Michael behind the turret of a mini-gun that had somehow appeared out of the roof of the SUV. I blinked in shock before once again Simon was pulling me forward and we were scrambling low to the ground toward the protection of the modified vehicle. We didn't stop moving until we'd rolled under neath its carriage and I took a second to stare at the chaos.

"Where's Sybil?" I couldn't see anything with the dust from the bullets hitting the ground mere inches from our faces.

"It doesn't matter where Sybil is. When Micheal gives the signal we need to get inside and get the hell out of here." Simon's eyes were trained on the mayhem surround us, waiting for Micheal's sign. I scrambled towards the tire that had been closest to where I'd seen Sybil and Sergei last, trying to make out where they had gone, or if she was even still alive.

"I have to find her. She can't escape."

Simon gripped my arm so hard it almost hurt, and I whipped my head around to look at him.

"Hannah, she's gone. You lost yer chance. Right now, we have to get out of here or we're all dead. Micheal and Evan can only hold them off so long." His voice was hoarse, his accent thicker than I remembered. But more than that, he sounded and looked angry. Something about his tone and the look on his face, as if I was to blame for the mess we were in, set me off and I snarled.

"Fuck that. I didn't come all this way to let her get away *again.*" I started to scramble out from the protection of the Hummer and its thick tires, but he managed to grab the collar of my jacket and yanked me back before pinning me to the ground with his weight. Even as beat up and covered in blood as he was, the heavy weight of him still sent thrills through my body and I flushed in response.

"Are you mad, lass?" He snarled in my face as his body pressed into mine, causing my heart to race. "We are in no position to attack. You waltzed into a death trap and pulled my team with you. Now we're going to have to get out of here on a hope and a prayer. I'll no' put you or them in harm's way for anyone. No' again."

I stared at him for a few breaths, a mix of rage and desire burning through me, as I realized he was right. Even more so when more bullets struck the side of our vehicle and Micheal banged on the roof. "Quit playing turtle and get your asses inside!"

He stared down at me for a few seconds more, anger burning off him in waves, before he grunted and scooted to the side, allowing me to roll to my belly and slither after him.

"On my signal..." He growled and then as Michael laid down more cover fire he shouted "Now!" and rolled out from under the SUV, reaching up to open the door. At the same time the door was flung open, he reached down and half hauled, half dragged me out from under the vehicle before pushing me forward and into the passenger seat. I scrambled across the leather and center console to the driver's side and immediately threw it in reverse as more bullets slammed into the windshield.

When Michael had said he'd taken care of our transportation arrangements, I hadn't realized we'd be in what was basically one step down from an upright armored vehicle. But somehow I wasn't surprised. It was exactly the kind of over the top badassery I was coming to expect from this team of Ghosts. Simon slammed the door closed just as I jammed down on the gas and screamed at Michael to hold on to his balls.

As I watched people scrambling out of our way in my rearview mirror, I remembered the van that had maneuvered to block us in.

"Shit," I muttered and slammed on the brakes. Simon went flying forward, hitting the dash, and gave me a dirty glare, to which I only said, "Put on your seat belt." And then called out to Micheal. "Hey buddy, we need that van moved or we aren't going anywhere." But before I could even finish my sentence, I heard a distinct whoosh, whine, and then the whole vehicle shook as something exploded behind us.

Wild-eyed, I turned to look at Simon. "Who the *fuck* are you people? And how the *fuck* did Michael get a grenade launcher? No, you know what? I don't want to know. I do *not* want to know." And then I shoved the shifter into drive before slamming on the gas again and whipped the SUV around towards the smoldering remains of the van that Micheal had just incinerated.

Gravel and dirt went flying as the tires squealed and we barreled towards the entrance. More bullets bounced off the hood of the vehicle and I swore as a few of Sybil's men moved to blockade us again, their weapons firing directly at our engine and tires in an attempt to take them out. I hoped that along with the machine gun attachment and bullet proof glass Micheal had the foresight to upgrade to run-flat tires and a rein-forced engine compartment.

"Keep going." Simon growled next to me, as if sensing my hesitation and reluctance to just run people over, even if those people were trying to kill us. I looked over to see him putting the finishing touches on assembling a AR-15 and then he lowered his window to begin returning fire while Micheal continued to cover our rear. The men in front of us quickly realized they were either going to become road kill or bullet fodder, and jumped out of the way. Then Simon pulled back inside and quickly rolled his window back up.

"Jesus christ do you guys just pull weapons out of your ass?"

The SUV hit a bump in the road dirt road hard as we exited the clearing and Simon grabbed hold of the oh shit handle, giving me a glare, as if the quality of the ride was somehow my fault. "No, we keep them in the dash. Are you sure you know how to drive this?"

I snorted and whipped the SUV around another sharp turn, glancing down at the pre-programmed map on the display screen. "I told you to put on a seatbelt."

Rue's soft accent filled my ear once again. "Evan and I are at the extraction point. You've got incoming from the east and it looks like they're trying to cut you off."

"Great, just great. Do I have another route?" I glanced at Simon, worry now combining with my fear. He looked pale and was half slumped in the seat, beads of sweat lining his forehead. "Rue, tell Evan to get the med kit ready. Si doesn't look so good."

Simon sat up and shook his head. "I'm fine, lass. Just pay attention to the road and get us out of here."

"Are you shot? You're covered in blood." I saw the

map update as Rue recalculated our exit route and winced. "Hold on, this is going to get bumpy," I glanced over at him,"... er..."

Simon flinched, but gave me a grim smile. "No, I'm not shot. It's not my blood, mostly." The way he said those words sent chills down my spine, and I was both relieved and worried at the same time. What had Sybil done to him in these weeks? What had they had forced him to do?

I heard a thump and a thud as Micheal banged on the roof of the SUV. "I see them coming. Get ready!"

Sure enough, in my side mirror, I saw the dust from tires as two pickup trucks raced towards us. I looked over at Simon again. "You ready?"

Something of the old Simon returned as he gave me a cocky smirk, "For you princess? Always."

"Good to know." I quipped back and then whipped the wheel around and yelled at Michael to hold on. We shot off the road and into a farmer's freshly harvested field. The ground was soft from rain and I prayed to Saint Michael that we wouldn't end up stuck and in need of a second rescue.

Ahead of us, I could make out the low roofs of our extraction point. Behind us, dirt flew up as the two trucks tried to follow and Michael continued to spray bullets, keeping them from coming any closer.

I looked over at Simon, who looked like he was one

second away from passing out. "Si, when we get to the extraction point, you're going to need to hit the ground running. Do you understand?" He didn't open his eyes but just nodded his head once and fear gripped my heart.

"Simon Gallagher I mean it. Do *not* pass out on me now. I didn't come all this way just to leave your irritating ass behind."

He snorted then and opened his eyes. "Don't you mean you came for your stolen evidence?"

I frowned but didn't respond. Now was not the time to discuss motives.

And then we were barreling through a low fence that surrounded the abandoned barn where Rue and Evan were waiting for us. I slammed on the emergency brake and the SUV came to a screeching halt. We had mere seconds to get to the helicopter that was waiting for us, but even over the whir of the blades that were starting up, I could hear the shouts and the bullets from the men pursuing us.

"Michael! Get Simon!" I shouted and opened up my door just as Michael jumped down from the roof and went for Simon's door, pulling him out and grabbing him by the waist as he half carried him towards the waiting helicopter. I grabbed the AR-15 that Simon had left in his seat before jumping out to follow behind him as Rue shouted at us. But her words were carried away by the sound of the blades.

Michael and Simon reached the helicopter deck just seconds before I did, even as more bullets began whizzing around us. I grabbed the nearest thing I could hold on to as I felt the massive bird begin to lift and pulled myself up. Rue reached down to drag me the last few inches inside and I collapsed onto the floor as she slammed the door closed. The ting of bullets bouncing off the propellors and hull matched the erratic beating of my heart.

I glanced up to see Simon staring at me from where he was propped against one wall of the helicopter. His face was like stone, hard and unreadable. But his eyes, oh his eyes, they glittered with unspoken emotion and I swallowed, suddenly more anxious than I'd been the entire time we'd been under pursuit. Because I knew, without a shadow of a doubt, that Simon Gallagher was pissed. And I knew why.

CHAPTER NINE

Simon

I watched the Bay of Finland come into view under the cover of darkness, dark water lapping against the large cruise ships docked there and frowned. My thoughts were just as dark as the freezing water hundreds of feet below us. The helicopter was too noisy for conversation so all of my questions swirled around in a maelstrom that clouded my thoughts for the entirety of our flight.

But both Michael and Rue had hovered over me like mother hens the minute we'd safely gotten into air and confirmed that we weren't going to be pursued. After convincing them I was fine and in no danger of bleeding out on anytime soon, I'd spent the rest of flight observing the woman across from me.

She hadn't looked my way once since collapsing in her seat, AR-15 slung over her ripped jeans as a booted foot tapped nervously, eyes never leaving the ground as it disappeared beneath us. I took in every smudge of dirt, every spatter of blood on her clothes, the dark circles under her eyes. Anger and guilt warred inside of me. Anger because I'd dragged her into this mess. Guilt because I felt like I was betraying the woman who'd set me on this path.

The memory of Tory's face as she died came back to me, her blue eyes full of shocked betrayal as the light had faded from them. I turned away from Hannah, no longer able to look at her. What would she say if she knew what I'd done? What kind of man would she say I was? I'd already betrayed her once and proven I was ruthless in pursuing my target. Maybe if she knew the truth, she'd do what she should have done in the first place, and run. My jaw clenched painfully as somewhere inside of me, I acknowledged I wasn't so sure I'd be able to let that happen. Hannah might want to run, but I didn't know if I could let her go.

My dark thoughts and exhaustion blocked out much of what was going on around me and the next thing I knew Michael was tapping me on the shoulder and we were exiting the bird to a waiting blacked out

SUV on a small tarmac. I looked around for Hannah, but somehow she'd slipped away when I wasn't looking.

"She's not here." Michael's gruff voice pulled my attention away from searching for her.

He slipped into the driver's seat, giving one snarling glare to the company driver who'd started to object, but then quickly scrambled out of the way to let the hulking man take over.

"Where is she?" I noticed that neither Evan nor Rue seemed to be concerned with her absence as they both slid into their own seats and I settled down, trying to keep my voice neutral.

Rue cast a quick glance to Evan before she cleared her throat and gave me a small smile. "She didn't tell us."

I glared, the tension palpable in the vehicle. "What do you mean, she didn't tell you?"

"She may have helped us find you Si, but Hannah isn't one of us." Michael growled from the front seat.

It was Rue's turn to glare at Michael. "She did more in a few days than we could do in weeks."

Michael met her gaze in the rearview mirror and looked like he wanted to retort, but instead, just shook his head and stayed quiet. I looked at Evan, who was sitting next to Michael in the front seat. "Are you going to play ignorant on this, too?"

Evan turned to look at me and I observed the face

of my best and oldest friend. "Hannah doesn't owe us anything, Si," was all he said before turning back around and going silent as well.

Frustration and confusion burned through me. "What the fuck has been going on?"

Michael glanced at me again in the rearview and sighed, some of the anger he held inside dissipating. "You're going to have to ask Hannah that one. I might not like it, but Rue and Evan are right. Hannah did more to locate you in a couple of days than we'd had luck with in weeks. And what she did to do it, or why, is her business. When we asked for her help, that was the agreement. We did it on her terms and we didn't ask questions."

I sat back in my seat, suddenly understanding the tension from Evan and Rue, and the anger from Micheal. None of them liked not being in the loop when it came to information. I could only imagine how Hannah had come in and upended their way of doing things. But from what I gathered, they did it willingly and had followed her lead.

"So you're telling me that three of the best damn mercenaries in the business got their tits handed to them by a federal agent from Georgia?"

I watched as Micheal's jaw ticked with frustration and felt a sudden burst of pride as he said, "I told Rue we would have found you, eventually."

To Rue's credit, she didn't respond, just muttered in French under her breath and looked out the window. Michael's eyes narrowed and growled softly, "Say that again, little kitten, and I'll hold you to it." I arched a brow in question as a pretty blush spread across Rue's cheeks and I decided then and there that I was glad I didn't understand more than "Bon jour". Although I was a little surprised that Michael did. In all the years we'd worked together, he'd never spoken it. But, as much as I didn't want to acknowledge it, there were still things about the broody ex-special forces operator that I didn't know. I'd learned to keep my questions to myself though, Michael had proven himself and his loyalty more than once to this team. If there was something he wanted to keep private, I would not be the one to pry it out of him.

We pulled up to a hotel just outside of Helsinki's wharf area. It was late, and the streets were blessedly empty, but in the distance I could see the bright lights of the cruise ships glittering on the water. Much like the streets outside, the hotel wasn't remarkable. The lobby was empty and the lone desk attendant paid little attention to our rag-tag group limping towards the elevators.

"So, no one can tell me where our little southern belle may have disappeared? Or who she's meeting with?" Suspicion lingered in my voice. I knew she couldn't have just walked away from the bureau without making some serious concessions or worse, going rogue. The thought of that made my stomach twist. Whatever the cost to her career, I vowed I would be the one to pay it. I still had strings to pull with some higher ups in a few three letter agencies in the states and I'd use whatever bribes, threats, or violence if necessary to see that she was protected. And if someone was threatening her to get to me? There wouldn't be a hole dark or deep enough for them to hide from me.

I spoke as we stepped out of the elevator into the hall just as a door directly across from it opened and the hellion herself was standing there, a white towel wrapped around her head and draped in a matching hotel robe, looking freshly showered and not at all at the mercy of some nefarious handler. She shot me a cocky grin, emerald green eyes glittering as they nailed me to where I was standing. "Simon, haven't you ever heard of 'Need to know'?" I swallowed, suddenly confronted with her beauty like a punch in a gut.

I felt Michael pat my shoulder reassuringly and Evan snicker softly as they all moved around where I was rooted to step inside the room. She moved so they could squeeze by her, not taking her eyes off me for a long moment. And then, without another word, she just turned and moved away from the door, leaving it wide open. Leaving me a choice. It only took me half a second to make up my mind. If this was the game Hannah wanted to play, then fine, I would play, even if it destroyed us both.

Crossing the threshold, I let the door shut behind me and took in the scene for a minute. Micheal was over at a small table he'd set up as a makeshift bar, pouring a glass of whiskey. Evan had dropped onto a leather sofa in front of a TV and was lazily flipping through euro channels looking for a fut ball match. Rue had already flipped open her laptop, the blue light reflecting off her smooth caramel skin as she skimmed whatever dark channels and chats she was constantly monitoring. It looked exactly like a scene from any number of post-mission wrap-ups. The team separating to decompress before we'd come back together to after action review everything and go over any missing details or information.

I stepped further into the room and was about to cross over to Rue to begin the debrief when one of the two doors adjoining the room opened and Hannah stepped back into the suite. The robe and towel were gone, now replaced by black yoga pants and a t-shirt that had a picture of Spok from Star Trek and the words "Live Long and Prosper" scrawled across it. Every inch of her curvy body was outlined and seeing her like that, fresh and innocent looking, made my blood boil and suddenly the rage I'd been keeping under check for the past several hours boiled over.

"Glad your shower was so important that you couldn't let anyone know where the fuck you were." The words were out of my mouth before I could snatch them back. I saw her flinch, eyes flaring for a moment before they narrowed and she crossed her arms under her chest, only enhancing the fact that she definitely wasn't wearing a bra underneath. My mouth went dry, my cock went hard and for some reason, that made me even angrier.

"I'm sorry Simon. You don't understand the situation. I'm no longer your asset. In fact, the only "ass" I am to you is the one who saved *yours.*" Her chin notched up slightly as the room went deadly silent, the other members of my team seeming to have stopped breathing as they watched the showdown between us.

"It's not my ass I care about, *princess.*" I growled her nickname like it was a bitter taste on my tongue, even as my balls tightened as I thought about how delicious her ass was. "It's the people you put in danger because you're stove-piping information." Now that I'd started, I couldn't stop and the words pour out of me.

"My team may have come to you for help, but keeping secrets and going off like a lone-ranger just puts them in more danger. Danger they didn't ask for. You don't want to tell me what you're up to or who you're meeting with? Fine." It wasn't fine though. The idea of her meeting with a secret handler made my stomach twist. I stalked closer to her. "I know exactly what,"need to know" means, lass." Echoing her words to me from weeks ago. "But if anyone in this room needs to know something, it's you."

Stubbornness flashed in her emerald eyes and she didn't budge even as I towered over her, covered in blood and probably smelling exactly like I felt. Total shit. "And exactly what do I need to know, Si?"

"That Sybil was right. You're in over your fucking head, princess. Now if you'll excuse me, I'm going to clean up. *Some* of us haven't actually showered in a few weeks." And then I pushed past her before I could feel guilty over the look of pity that had briefly crossed her face. Or admit that the person I was really furious with was myself.

CHAPTER TEN

Hannah

I stood there for a moment, just staring at the door that he'd slammed closed after pushing me to the side. I had expected a lot of things from seeing Simon again. Guilt wasn't one of them. And yet it was there, written in every word he said, and every glance he'd given me over the long flight back to Helsinki. In the cramped helicopter, I'd done everything I could to avoid looking at him while I warred with my own emotions. But his eyes had burned into me just like they always did and when we'd landed, I'd taken the momentary distraction to slip away.

I'd needed to report back to my counterpart in the city and then call to let my superiors know that the mission had been a semi-success. Although I don't think they considered it much of one. They weren't happy to hear that Sergei and Sybil had given us the slip and the underlying threat in Agent Reed's voice when he ended the phone call had my stomach in knots. "You have one mission, Agent Kelly. Don't forget that."

I turned towards the team and tried to calm my features. But they just observed me with the cool distance that had been between us since we'd begun working on finding Simon. "Oh please, so you're going to tell me you agree with him? You knew when you asked me to help that things would be done my way."

Michael just snorted and took a sip of the whiskey he'd poured before crossing the floor to the other door that led into an adjoining suite. "All I know is that for someone who gave us such shit about not being honest, looks like the kettle just called the pot black." Then, for a second time in a matter of minutes, a door slammed, and I flinched. God save me from alpha men and their sensitive egos.

Evan's icy gaze was unreadable. He held my stare for just a moment longer before going back to flipping channels until he found the match he wanted and I knew it would have been useless to talk to him, anyway. Still, ever since that evening at the coffee shop in Turkey, he hadn't spoken much. Just offered his thoughts on how to best execute our mission. In-fact the only person of the three, Rue, had been the only one to offer more than a cursory comment or opinion.

I sighed and sat down at the table next to her where she'd paused her scrolling for a moment to glance at me and then returned right back to her screen. I frowned, suddenly feeling like my only ally might not actually be on my side anymore. "You *do* remember calling me for my help, right?"

Rue nodded but didn't lookup. "Oui, I called you."

"And so now I'm supposed to feel like I'm a part of this team because we completed a mission together?"

Rue shrugged, her face impassive. "You can feel however you want to feel Mon Cher. No one is holding you here now."

I flinched at her words. "What so you're saying you've gotten what you want from me, I can go?" Anger tinged my words.

She finally raised her amber gaze to meet mine and whatever anger I was feeling quickly dissolved into guilt. "What other reason would you have to stay?" My mouth went dry.

Leaning forward, I whispered earnestly, "I'm not here to betray you, Rue." She arched a perfectly sculpted brow. "I never said you were, Hannah." The weight of her words was on my shoulders as I sat back. "I want to get Sybil and Sergei as much as you do. Maybe more now."

She didn't say anything for a few breaths, just stared at me in a way that reminded me eerily of Simon, and I realized how close they really were. "Then maybe you want to be a part of this team after all, no?" Her silky French accent held a bit of amusement, but then she turned back to her browsing, effectively dismissing me.

I sat at the table for a few moments longer, my thoughts racing, and then stood up with a tired sigh before moving towards the door Simon had disappeared through. I hadn't bothered to try to let him know that his room was actually across the hall with Michael, but now that it was late and I was exhausted, I fully planned on kicking him out so I could get some rest.

Or at least that was the way the conversation went in my head. All coherent thought left though when I stepped into the room and saw him silhouetted against the bathroom door frame as steam from his shower billowed around him. A flush went through me I knew had nothing to do with the muggy air from the shower and everything to do with the half naked man in front of me.

He moved away from the door, the towel he'd used to dry his hair draped over one shoulder, a second towel was wrapped around his waist and I didn't want to let my eyes drop to the dip of his hips as it slipped down them just a tad.

After weeks of torture, his bruised and broken skin stretched across tight muscles, but it did nothing but make him look leaner and more dangerous. Like a blade that had been sharpened and bloodied. Those muscles pulled and bunched as he stalked across the room, not caring that he was practically naked. Heat pooled low in my belly as he came closer. Jesus, this man did things to me.

I cleared my throat, attempting to speak and take control of my thoughts, but he interrupted me.

"Ye came for me..." the growl of his voice and the sound of his accent sent a pulse of pleasure right down to my core and I bit my lip. Apparently, the shower had done little to help him cool his temper because his eyes were still blazing with a mix of anger, guilt and... lust? I swallowed thickly as I noticed the obvious bulge behind the towel that wasn't doing a very good job of hiding.

I tipped my chin up and crossed my arms under my chest. "I came for Sybil too. Is that what you spent your shower time thinking about? Don't you ever have like, shower thoughts or something?" I had a sudden image of Simon naked in the shower, soap and water dripping down his hard abs, his fist wrapped around his thick member.

He ignored my attempt to deflect the conversation. "You recruited my team. You kidnapped Sergei. Infiltrated a terrorist organization. Then orchestrated an attack on their operations, all to trade him so that ye could get to *me*." He punctuated each statement with a step closer until he was towering over me and I realized he was practically vibrating with barely contained fury. I licked my lips and his eyes zeroed in on them, darkening even more.

"First of all, your team recruited *me*. And second, I knew that Sybil would never give you or herself up unless I had leverage. The only thing I've *ever* seen Sybil show an ounce of care for was Sergei. I knew I needed him."

Grey orbs flicked away from my mouth and back to me. "Aye, and how did that work out for you, princess? Hmm? Because as I see it, not only do you not have Sybil, but you don't have Sergei, either." His gravelly voice snarled, and I flinched at the sight of scratches and bruises around his neck. "I was tortured and beaten for *weeks* in order to bring them down and now I'm standing here, *right as rain,* and *they are out there free to destroy more lives. Because of you.*" His voice was a quiet roar of fury and suddenly I snapped, leaning in even closer to him. I wasn't going to let his man-sized temper tantrum distract from the truth.

"Is that it, Simon? You're mad that you're still here and breathing? Because from where I'm standing, I'm looking at a dead man, anyway." He snarled, but didn't interrupt me. "Or is your guilt eating you alive so much that you're trying to distract yourself with fake outrage?" He flinched slightly at my words and I knew I had him.

"Did you think getting captured and tortured by Sybil was going to make up for killing Victoria and using me? Did you think *dying* while bringing down their organization was going to absolve you of all your sins?"

Surprise flashed through his grey eyes at the mention of Victoria's name, and I nodded. "Yeah, buddy, I know all about your little vendetta against my sister and Sergei. And I'm by no means saying that I forgive you for the shit you pulled by lying to me or tricking me into getting you close to Sybil, but I am going to say I get it."

Some of the fight seemed to leave him, but his body was still coiled like a cobra ready to strike.

"I'm not upset that I'm alive, Hannah."

I scoffed and rolled my eyes. "Oh please, Si. You're telling me you got yourself caught and *expected* to just walk out of there with all body parts intact?"

He shook his head and leaned down further, our noses practically touching as fury and something else darkened his gaze. "You don't fecking get it, do you, lass? This is my job. This is my life and my mission. I'm always prepared to not be able to walk away. But you?

It's not your job, Hannah. None of this. Aye, I made a mistake. But not in killing Victoria. Victoria was dead long before my bullet ever found her. It just took me too long to realize it."

His hand came up to cup the side of my face, his thumb tracing my bottom lip, and suddenly the heat that I'd felt earlier turned into a raging flame as lust and that thing I didn't want to acknowledge rushed through me.

"No, lass, I'm mad that you were put in harm's way for me. For any of this. And I'm pissed that I'm the one who set you on this path in the first place. I should never have lied to you, Hannah. I should never have tried to use you. I was so blinded by my mission, my revenge, that I almost got you killed. And for that, I'll never forgive myself."

CHAPTER ELEVEN

Hannah

I had no words. They were lost just like the sense my Memaw said I never had and the next thing I knew, my mouth was on his and I was kissing him with like I was starved. A low groan filled the air between our lips as my hand came up to tangle in his wet hair. I could feel his hard length behind the towel that somehow had the indecency to stay in place despite my best effort to grind it from between us.

The kiss was like a match to gasoline. His lips, so firm and demanding, moved devoured mind, and I pressed myself closer to him, wanting to invade his soul just as much as he'd invaded my own.

Suddenly, I heard a sharp hiss of pain, and he pulled

away. I started to question him, but then the realization hit that I was practically trying to climb a man who had at least half a dozen broken ribs and possibly a concussion. Feeling slightly chagrined, I took half a step back, trying to catch my breath and slow the racing of my heart.

"I'm sorry, you're hurt and probably should get some rest. I'll tell Evan to take a look at your ribs." I turned to leave, determined to save some face. What had I been thinking, to just kiss him like that? Especially after everything that had happened between us. Hell, had he even wanted to kiss me? But then I felt a strong hand on the back of my neck and the next thing I knew I was being pulled back against a muscular chest as his voice growled into my ear, "If you think I'm letting you walk out of that door after I've done nothing but think about what you taste like, feel like, then we're going to find out very quickly if spanking is indeed your kink of choice."

I gasped as he turned me around. He let the towel fall to the floor, and I took my time dragging my gaze over every inch of him, wincing at the evidence of Sybil's handiwork that cross-crossed his body before taking in the sight of his thick cock and the lust I'd felt just a few moments ago raged to life again. Trailing my hands down his chest and I peered up at him with a smirk. "Simon, you might be better than James Bond, but you're only human. You've got at least half a dozen cracked ribs and God knows what other injuries. I don't think you're in the best medical condition to be determining what my kinks are or aren't."

The arrogant look that all men got when they felt like their masculinity was being challenged flashed across his face and he seemed about to argue with me, but then I was slowly sliding down to my knees, removing my t-shirt as I did so.

"So I'm just going to skip to it and show you one of them."

And then I was sliding my lips over the tip of his cock and moaning in satisfaction. I loved the silky feel of the skin against my lips and tongue as my mouth moved further down his length and then peeked up from under my lashes to see him staring down at me in awe and wonder.

I took my time drawing back and slowly increased the suction as my tongue swirled under the shaft, which won me a groan, "Jesus Christ, Hannah..."

I moaned with encouragement as his hands came to my hair and he rocked against my mouth, matching the rhythm that I set until I sped up and grabbed his hips, pulling him harder against me. With one last questioning look down at me, he took the hint and surged his hips forward with a punishing speed, his cock sliding into my mouth with long strokes.

Wetness pooled between my thighs and I shifted only slightly so that I could slide my fingers down the front of my yoga pants and rub my aching clit. Suddenly, he pulled me off of him with a growl and tugged me to my feet.

"I didn't spend all those nights dreaming of your pussy just to get my dick sucked without so much as a taste."

I started to protest about his ribs again until he moved to the bed and laid down, slowly stroking his hand up and down his spit-soaked cock. "Strip and come sit on my face."

I grinned with delight. "Someone is a little bossy, aren't they?" But I was rolling my pants down and over my hips before slowly climbing onto the bed between his legs. His eyes grew darker, the pupils so dilated his irises were nearly black. I could see it then, the edge that he rode so hard. Something in me wanted to see what happened when all that beautiful discipline vanished and it was just Simon, wild and untamed.

"Aye, and someone isn't listening very well. I said I wanted to taste you, lass."

I gave a long teasing stroke of my tongue up his length before dipping down to pull one of his balls into my mouth, rolling it around my tongue with a satisfied hum. "Hannah..." he growled. The next thing I knew, I felt the sharp smack of his hand on my ass cheek and I sat up. "Hey!" He glared. "You're testing my limits, lass." I wanted to protest but thought better of it as he tried to hide the pain sitting up so fast to reach me had caused him. This might not be the right time to tell him spanking was definitely on the "not a kink" list.

Instead, I moved languidly up the length of his body before twisting and straddling my thighs on both sides of his head. I held myself aloft for the barest of seconds until I felt his hot breath on my core and the sweep of his tongue through my folds. "Fecking delicious..." he growled against my core before pulling my hips down and back to give him a better angle.

Pleasure spiked through me as I felt his tongue circle against my clit before latching on and suckling.

"Oh, god...." I groaned and rocked against his face. He pulled away just the slightest and gave me a gentle push on my lower back. "Not god baby, but you taste like heaven."

His words had me ready to melt all over him. But I wasn't done enjoying myself and I leaned down to take his thick length down my throat again, careful to keep my weight off his chest and ribs. We found a rhythm quickly, with him guiding my hips over his mouth and face so that I could suck and tease his cock in tandem. I stroked and squeezed his thickness, loving how hard and smooth he felt in my grip, as my tongue flicked the salty tip before once again swallowing him whole.

He growled, hips thrusting as I allowed him to press himself as far down my throat as I could handle. At the same time, his thick fingers plunged into my wetness, filling me in a way that made me ache with desperation. The pleasure built until I wasn't sure how much more I could handle, and I whimpered with need.

"Aye, lass, that's it. Come on my fingers while I come down your throat." His words vibrated against my pussy and I hummed around him in response. "Fuck Hannah, you feel and taste so good." And then his mouth was on my clit again while his fingers continued a punishing rhythm that matched the flicking of his tongue against me. The orgasm ripped through me so hard and fast that I cried out with my release, but it died quickly as his own orgasm exploded and I swallowed hard as he pumped down my throat.

I collapsed on the bed beside him, breathless and panting, the taste of him a lingering tanginess on my tongue. I had never experienced something so intense just from oral sex before. I'd always enjoyed it, but not like this. Which was a shame, because both giving and receiving head was a favorite of mine. Unfortunately, most men wanted to do all the receiving and none of the giving. They treated pleasuring a woman it like it was the optional side dish on a dinner menu. But not

Simon. No, Simon had devoured me like I was a five-course meal, and he was going back in for seconds.

I felt his weight shift, and I rolled over to look at him. His eyes were closed, his breaths steady and even, which told me he'd fallen asleep. For the first time since he'd come into my life, I saw him relaxed and at peace, and I frowned. As much as I didn't want to admit it, he was right. I was in over my head. I was in over my head with Sybil. I was in over my head with Agent Reed. I was in over my head with the whole Abromov business. But more importantly, as the after-glow of my orgasm faded and exhaustion forced my eyes to close, I realized I was in over my head with Simon Gallagher.

Hannah

Warm sunlight danced through the half-closed curtains and, for a few brief seconds, I enjoyed the feel of it on my skin. Until I heard foreign voices outside my window and I came fully awake with a panicked start. After a few heart pounding moments of anxiousness, I realized it was merely the local crowd of shoppers that were wandering towards the wharf and the Helsinki market square. Flopping back down with a sigh, I rolled over to snuggle back into the warmth of the body I'd fallen asleep next to, but Simon was gone. I glared at the empty spot and rumpled sheets. Apparently, that warm body had gotten up earlier than me. It figured that even capture, torture, and a daring escape wouldn't be enough to make the rigid Simon Gallagher miss his early bird get's the worm routine.

Showering and dressing quickly, I pulled open the door that led to the living room suite, wondering if Evan had managed to snatch any of the delicious pullas from the hotel breakfast bar. One taste of the amazing cardamon sweetbread, drizzled in a sugar frosting, and I'd been hooked. I fully intended on hunting down the recipe to take back home to make. Or to have my mom make it for me. More than likely, I'd just burn down my apartment or have a dough explosion in the kitchen if I tried it on my own.

Mouth watering in anticipation of the wake up and kick ass combination of sugar and coffee, I stopped short at the sight in front of me. They had cleared the living room out with the small couch pushed against one wall and the table Rue had been working at, plus another they must have commandeered from the hotel lobby, pushed together in the middle. Laptops were open and screens were blinking with messages and satellite images on one side and on the other. A small arsenal of weapons was laid out in neat order. Evan and Micheal sat in front of the guns, meticulously checking the chambers and barrels, while loading clips full of ammo. Across the room, where Evan had been watching his fut ball match the night before, the TV had been taken off the wall and replaced with a full scale grid map and what looked like the architectural plans of a large house or compound.

I looked for Simon but didn't see him in the room, nor Rue, for that matter. Frowning, I walked over to the table to where Evan and Michael were inspecting and prepping their gear.

"Did someone call for a full scale assault or something? I'd really prefer to do that after coffee and breakfast, not before." The joke fell flat and a sick feeling was beginning to form in the pit of my stomach. Michael flicked his dark eyes towards me before casting them back down to the HK416 assault rifle he was currently cleaning and muttered, "Something like that."

I flinched and turned towards Evan. "Really?" I flicked a hand toward the wall. "Are we back to stonewalling information again? What's happening?"

Evan stayed quiet and didn't even bother looking up at me. I growled with frustration, running fingers through my hair as I resisted the urge to punch the two neanderthals in their pretty faces. "Well, can I at *least* get a cup of coffee before we start planning another mission? Another mission *no one* has filled me in on, by the way?"

"Here's yer coffee, lass." Simon's gravelly voice made me snap my head towards the door where I saw him standing in the entryway holding a tray of coffee and Rue beside him with a bag of what I hoped was delicious pastries. "But *you*, Agent Kelly, aren't planning anything. You're going home."

The finality in his voice hit me like a ton of bricks. So we were back to this then. Never mind the earth shattering orgasms we'd shared or the way he'd growled my name like it was a prayer last night. I should have known that this was all it would ever be to him. Simon Gallagher had told me time and time again that nothing stood between him and his mission. And despite his new found conscious and guilt over using me to get to my sister, it looked like that part of him would never change.

I fought to overcome the wave of emotions that threatened to overwhelm me. My sister's face flashed in my mind and I could just hear her smug voice whisper, *"Didn't I tell you he'd break your heart?"*

When I could finally unclench my jaw enough to speak, it was to Rue, not Simon. "So I guess this means I'm definitely not part of the team." Rue had the decency to look chagrined but just pressed her lips together in a firm line.

"As I told you before, Cherie, only you can decide that." Inwardly I flinched at her words but raised my chin a notch, not wanting them to see how much I was hurt or the other swirling emotions my own conscious was pressing down on me.

"So what, you brought coffee and pastries as some sort of peace offering? Here, thanks for saving our asses and rescuing our leader and oh yeah, tracking down the operations of a hidden organization that we've been hunting for *years*. But I'm sure this sack of calories will make up for your time well spent."

Simon stepped forward, and I couldn't help but notice how much a good night's rest and food had done for him. Freshly shaven, with his dark hair slicked back and a new leather jacket hugging his broad shoulders, I was reminded of the man I'd met so many weeks ago in my interrogation room. The man who with one touch and one word had made my head spin from the moment I'd met him. The one who had feasted on me like I was a meal he couldn't get enough of. Only now it seemed like he'd had his fill. Something in my chest tightened.

"Ye knew this would happen, lass‑"

"Don't call me fucking lass, Simon." He paused, frowning, but nodded.

"You knew this would happen, Agent Kelly." The pressure in my chest intensified to the point of actual pain. He used my name. Not lass, not princess, not even Hannah. It was Agent Kelly. Inwardly, I scoffed at the irony that after all his posturing, flirting, and over‑bearing ways, he was finally deciding to put up a professional wall between us. *"You knew this would happen, Hannah. Who would love you?"* Red fiery rage flared.

"You're not prepared for what we need to do. *You* weren't meant to go this far." I saw a moment of guilt flash across his features before they hardened once more. So that's what this was. Simon was trying to atone for his sins again.

"What do you mean 'prepared for what we need to do'?" The phrase raised alarm bells, and I turned towards the large map on the wall and then back down to the table of weapons where Micheal and Evan had paused their layout to watch the showdown between us. Realization dawned like a stone in the pit of my stomach turning it sour.

"You found them."

Simon didn't say anything, just continued to stand there, steam billowing from the tray of coffee mugs he held.

"You found them and you're going after them." I cocked my head, waiting for him to speak, but the cold grey eyes in-front of me didn't flinch, just reflected my image back at me.

"You son of a bitch. You're going to kill her."

Simon set the coffee down slowly on the table. Whether it was because he was tired of holding it or because he thought I might be inclined to throw the scalding hot bean juice in his face, I wasn't sure. What he didn't know was that I'd never waste good coffee like that.

"You have a flight leaving tonight at 1800. I've already contacted a friend in the Bureau and they're going to take a look at your file and see what they can do to get you transferred somewhere else, somewhere safe."

I scoffed, "Don't you dare pretend like this is to keep me safe, Simon Gallagher. This is for your own sense of guilt and regret. You don't care about me, you just care about how you feel, what you want. And so long as you don't have to worry about anyone else's feelings, you can get carte blanche do whatever the fuck you like." I took a step forward, rage building with every word I spoke.

"I'm doing this for *you,* Hannah."

I scoffed, "Right, keep telling yourself that, buddy, whatever helps you sleep better at night. But just remember, I'm the one who found you. I'm the one who found my sister." I pointed at the map. "You think just because you got some intel on a compound that you can come in there and raid it without her finding out? How many times has Sybil outsmarted you?" I looked around at the entire team this time, letting them see not just my anger, but my hurt. Because yea, for some reason, this hurt. Never mind that I had my own guilt I was warring with internally, but a part of me had felt like I was a part of something. Back at the office, we had teams and partners, but outside of David, it was always a constant battle to prove myself. No one wanted to admit that the sometimes a woman had bigger balls than half the men in the room.

But not here, not with Rue and Evan and Micheal. And not even with Simon. He'd included me in everything when we first started our mission planning for Stockholm. Had let me sit back and take charge when my knowledge was more in-depth than theirs. And I'd revelled in every moment of it. From the intelligence gathering to the execution, I'd felt the same sense of rightness that only ever came from seeing the bad guys finally put away. And that's when it hit me. I *wanted* to be a part of this team, even though I knew it was just a pipe dream. But for a moment, especially back in that Turkish alleyway, I'd felt what it might have been like to have a group of people who had your back at every turn.

I crossed my arms and shook my head. It didn't matter how much I wished for it, chasing that feeling of belonging wouldn't get me what I wanted, anyway. Not to mention, I had Agent Reed breathing down my neck and promises that I'd made and couldn't break. Not without risking my life and career. But still I would be damned, after everything, if they were going to send me home empty-handed.

"Sybil is going to hand you guys your asses and you know it."

It was Michael who spoke next, and what he said shocked me.

"I agree with her, Simon."

I whipped around to where the giant devil sat, his hands so casually resting on a table full of death and destruction as if he was sitting down to family dinner. Inky black eyes bored directly into mine and what I read there made my mouth go dry. It was an understanding and a promise. *Fuck this up and I will end you.* He continued on, "Sybil has always been one or two steps ahead of us. I, for one, am tired of being just close enough and then losing the scent. If she has a better plan or can get us closer to ending this, then I say let her stay."

My mouth gaped like a fish out of water before my jaw snapped shut and I turned back to where Simon was taking in the measure of his team, reading their expressions as if they were having a silent conversation. Whatever he saw there caused him to turn back around and sigh as something resembling resignation flashed across his features.

"Fine." His voice was cold, emotionless. Simon the mercenary was fully back in the driver's seat. "You can stay, but on one condition."

I gritted my teeth, wanting to snap at him again

that putting conditions on the person you needed most wasn't exactly the best way to accomplish a goal. But I remained silent. Provoking him wouldn't help me to stay and I couldn't exactly say that if I didn't deliver on my deal with Agent Reed, there wouldn't be an office transfer waiting for me when I got back to the states. Unless it was a 4ft by 6ft office of concrete and metal bars.

"Let me guess, we do things your way?" My voice sounded bitter, even to my ears.

He shook his head. "No, on this team, we don't things any*one* person's way." He looked pointedly at me before continuing on. "The condition is that when we go after Sybil, ye stay behind."

CHAPTER THIRTEEN

Simon

I expected her to argue and as I watched the dance of emotions play out on her face; I wished with everything in me she would. It would give me the ammo I needed to convince my team that she needed to go. None of them wanted to see her in harm's way and none of them trusted her enough to not interfere when we finally had the chance to take out her sister. Because for as much as Hannah was dead set on getting justice for what Sybil Kelly had done, she still wanted to bring her in alive. Which meant when the time came to pull the trigger, Hannah would be a liability, in more ways than one.

"Fine."

I tried not to show my shock.

"I'll stay behind. You guys have more experience with this." A hand waved towards the prep table. "...kind of thing, anyway. I'd probably just get in the way." And she moved to where I had set down the coffee cups, looking for the one with her name written on it.

A nagging suspicion swirled in my gut, but I wasn't prepared to question her on it further. Instead, I watched as she brought the cup to her lips and closed eyes in pure bliss, letting out a low moan that made my cock instantly hard. Last night with her had been on replay in my mind. So much so that instead of sleeping in like I probably should have done, I'd gotten out of bed intending to shower and see if my team was up and ready for their debriefing when Rue had barged in. Her eyebrows had shot up in surprise as she glanced first at me and then Hannah, who was still fast asleep, her naked back turned towards the door. When she'd looked back at me again, there was concern in her soft expression, but she pitched her voice just low enough for me to hear.

"There's been some chatter. We may have something, I came to tell Hannah."

I'd glanced back to the sleeping woman and for a brief moment considered waking her up with the information. But then turned back around. "I'll be out in five." Rue nodded and backed out without saying another word.

True to my timeline, I'd showered, shaved and dressed in under five minutes, then slipped out of the room, shutting the door silently behind me. My team had been waiting for me in a half circle with arms crossed and stoic expressions, but there was an underlying current of energy that I knew all too well. First, though, I'd have to answer some tough questions.

Michael had been the first to speak. "You ever pull a stunt like that again and I'll leave you to rot and die. Then I'll drag your ass back from hell just to leave you to rot and die all over again."

I couldn't help the smile. "Wouldn't I already be dead then?"

Michael snorted. "Maybe, or maybe you'll just wish you were dead."

I'd nodded, "Noted." before turning to Rue. "I'm assuming yer going to threaten me too?"

Rue'd just shaken her head and sighed, "Desole' mon pote', I don't have anything to say that you haven't already said to yourself." She gave me a hard stare. "Be careful Simon, you are playing a dangerous game."

"It's always been a dangerous game, Rue."

"Oui, but the stakes are much higher now." She'd then flicked a pointed glance past me to the door where Hannah lay sleeping, but didn't say anything else.

She didn't have to. The weight of her words sunk into my soul like stones. The stakes weren't just high because we were facing a dangerous threat. Going after Sybil had been personal at first. But in reality, bringing down the Abromov group would be a deep blow to the underground weapons deals that kept dictators, terrorists, and totalitarian regimes in power. If my personal vendetta against Sybil got in the way of the mission, then Hannah's most certainly would. And if I stood in Hannah's way again, there was no question in my mind that she'd never forgive me for it.

I met Evan's icy stare last, and I wasn't too proud to admit that I was afraid to see what I'd find there. I'd expected anger, hatred, or cold indifference. Of everyone on the team, Evan was my closest friend and also the one person who had the most reason to hate me for not following through on our mission in Stockholm. For the past three years, he'd hunted the Abromov group with a single-minded intensity that had rivaled my own. The jovial playboy persona he adopted might have fooled the rest of the team, but underneath I knew he was merely a hunter biding his time and once he'd caught his prey, there would be nothing to hold him back. Part of Evan had died along with Victoria back in that Syrian desert. Perhaps even a bigger part than the one that had died inside of me. A wave of emotion I couldn't describe gripped me as

Hannah's sultry green eyes flashed in my mind. Maybe that part of me wasn't as dead as I wanted to believe, and even as I thought it, guilt followed quickly behind. What would Evan think?

So when I saw him break out into the biggest shit-eating grin I'd ever seen, I felt shock and some of the weight I'd been carrying suddenly felt lifted.

"'Bout time you finally blew a load off and got some of that stick that's been shoved up your ass out."

Rue coughed and punched him in his arm. "E! Seriously? That's what you say to him after we've been literally worried sick for weeks? You want to do some caveman chest thumping over him getting laid?"

Evan shrugged and just continued to grin. "What? Simon's my best mate. Of course I'm happy for him. Getting his jollies off doesn't change the fact that we still have a mission to do. I'm just glad he finally learned he can be a human instead of a robot. I was beginning to think he'd forgotten how the ole sticks and stones worked. Thought I'd have to hire professional help if he didn't break his dry spell soon."

And just like that, the group had snickered, moving to the couch and chairs in the middle of the room and we'd fallen into the easy routine of reviewing the information that had been gathered over the past few weeks. I told them what I knew of Sybil's operations based on the limited interactions I'd had with her and

Mr. Ugly outside of their torture room. In turn, they shared how they'd convinced Hannah to help them when all their own efforts had led to dead ends. I shook my head when I heard how easy it had been for Hannah to draw her sister out into the open.

"So you're telling me I was right? Hannah really is Sybil's weakness?"

Evan had nodded and leaned forward, arms braced on his knees as he filled me in. "Oi, and not just her Achilles heel, but her entire persona seems to be based around destroying Hannah in whatever way she can. It's like a cat toying with a field mouse. Only Sybil has been sickeningly leaving Hannah alive to taunt and torture with mind-fuck games. And she's been doing it for years, mate. Years." Evan shook his head, disgust etched in every line of his face.

I'd frowned. The disgust he felt echoed in a sick pit in my stomach. I'd known that Sybil had a weird fascination with Hannah, but had chalked it up to sibling rivalry. I'd never imagined that it would reach the extent that it did. It only solidified my decision to get Hannah away from the situation and her sister as fast as possible.

After that Rue had revealed that a source had given her the location of a new deal, the Abromov group was going to be facilitating, presumably at Sergei's own personal compound.

"How credible is this source?"

Rue glanced at Michael, almost hesitatingly, but he said nothing, choosing to remain silent. Whatever Rue read in his expression, she must have felt like she had his permission because she turned back to me. "When we were trying to find out where Sybil had taken you, we exhausted every source we could. Michael asked his family for help."

My head snapped up at that revelation and I looked at Michael. "You called your family?"

He just shrugged, big shoulders moving in a way that belied the heaviness of the situation. "Yeah, I did."

"And what will they want in return?" Micheal's family wasn't something we talked about much, but I knew more than he revealed to most and I knew that the cost for their help was steep. It was a price he'd been avoiding paying for years now. I wouldn't have said he was in hiding from his family, but with how little he spoke about them and the lengths he went to prevent them from knowing his movements, made me certain that he wouldn't be dropping in for any family reunions any time soon.

He'd shrugged again and flipped the laptop that had been resting on the table in-front of us around to reveal the grainy security footage of a darkened restaurant with a distinct face in focus. Sergei Abromov. And across from him at a dining table with his head surrounded by a cloud of cigar smoke, a man who could have been Michael's twin if he was twenty something years younger. Genuine concern gripped me now. It was one thing to deal with weapons dealers and a psychotic scientist. It was entirely another thing to deal with the Italian mafia.

"What do they want in return for this information?"

Michael shook his head. "I don't know, Si, and honestly didn't ask. But I'm sure they will come to collect their," his lip curled in a sneer. "...*payment*, when they decide the time is right. A calling card home of sorts."

I knew what sort of hold Michael was referring to. Sons of the Italian mafia weren't allowed to stray too far from the *familia* and none had dared stray as far as Michael had. I could see it in the way his grip tightened on his knee and the tension around his eyes. He could feel the leash, or noose, tightening already. There was no way I was going to let them come for him and drag him back into their dark depths. Especially not because of a fool mistake I'd made.

"You don't have to owe them anything Mike, this was my fuck up. I'll pay the price." I'd told him and meant it. But he'd just shook his head and smirked in a way that eerily reminded me of the man on the laptop screen.

"Sorry there, Si, you don't have the right patronage to be able to pay them. Don't worry. I know how to handle the *Padrino*. He smells blood in the water and thinks it means weakness. He doesn't realize it's not mine." Deadly confidence in every word he spoke made me nod my head and not continue to argue. If anyone knew the inner mind of his Italian mob family, it was Michael. I would just be there for when they came for him, which they would, whether he wanted my help or not.

As I mused over Michael's family suddenly becoming a factor in our game, I watched Hannah as she huddled in the corner with Rue, her eyes trained on the laptop in front of her as Rue was quietly filling her in on the details of the information she'd discovered this morning. I didn't know what Hannah had promised to her higher ups in the bureau, but my gut told me that whatever it was, it would be costly.

Suddenly, green eyes looked up and met mine as if she somehow knew what I was thinking. Something passed between us in those few seconds and I knew, without a doubt, that whatever commitments or promises she'd made, she would follow through on them. Because, much like me, Hannah Kelly was all about the mission. And that's when it hit me and I felt the realization like a punch in the gut. Hannah was going to break my heart. And I'd let her.

CHAPTER FOURTEEN

Hannah

Hot water beat against my skin, and I relaxed into the warmth. The scent of jasmine and vanilla from my favorite shampoo filling the steamy shower and I sighed. After the morning meeting and Simon agreeing to let me stay, I'd spent the next few hours going over the intel reports with Rue before moving on to studying the map of the compound where supposedly Sergei and his contacts were meeting.

Without a doubt, it was a trap. Everything in me screamed Sybil had set this up purposely to lure Simon and me right into her spider web. But when I'd voiced my concerns, he'd merely pinned me with that icy stare. "Aye lass, it's a trap fer sure. But it's a trap only if we allow it to be one."

Since no one else had seemed to want to discuss the possibility any further, we moved on to mission prep and planning. This was where I'd remained quiet, only offering my thoughts or suggestions when I'd felt like it was needed or directly asked. I'd meant what I said when I was ok with them going on to the compound without me. This kind of thing was their bread and butter, not mine. I had no intention of being in the way and getting someone hurt, or worse, killed. But was I going to be sitting back, knitting scarves while they were on the ground doing all the dirty work? Fuck no. I had a plan. But first, I needed a shower to clear my head and thoughts.

Thoughts that kept straying dangerously close to a certain grey eyed assassin and the way his hands and tongue had felt on my body the night before. I groaned and tipped my head back, the water streaming over my face now as I inwardly cursed. It was pretty obvious why Simon didn't want me on this mission and why he kept trying to pack me up and send me home. And if I was honest with myself, I appreciated the way he was trying to put my safety first. It showed that he was truly remorseful and maybe cared about me more than he was letting on.

But fuck him for coming into my life with that *voice* and those *eyes* and the kind of confident swagger that absolutely *ruined* any other man for me. I truly didn't know what to do. I knew that if I continued on the path my heart and my vagina wanted to hop, skip, and run down, I'd end up falling hard. Harder than I'd ever fallen for anyone else before him. All good sense told me I should just leave. Pack it up, make up some excuse and hope Agent Reed bought it, but get the hell away from Simon and from the heartbreak that was coming.

But I couldn't do that anymore than I could stop my heart from yearning for more of Simon's voice growling in my ear. *"Yer mine lass."*

A heat that had nothing to do with the shower flooded through my body and I felt my pussy clench at the memory of his tongue dominating me, edging my release and then teasingly flicking through my folds in denial until I'd screamed in frustration and demanded he give me what I so desperately wanted. *Him.*

My hands traveled of their own accord, sliding against my wet skin and down toward the ache between my thighs. Damn him for twisting my body around just a few words and sexy growls. Damn him for being more honorable than I'd wanted to believe. And damn him for not following me back to the shower to fuck the thoughts out of my head and silence the words that kept swirling around. *"Who could love you, Hannah? Without me, you're nothing. You're MY Hannah."*

A sob caught in my throat even as I tried to chase the budding orgasm and my fingers slipped over my wet clit. Suddenly I felt a hand, firm and warm, cover mine as another came up to cup my face. My eyes flew open as solemn greys bored into mine. They flickered over my face, frowning when they saw tears form, threatening to spill.

He was standing with me in the shower, fully clothed, although his leather jacket and shoes had been left outside the shower door. Confusion must have shown on my face as I watched the white t-shirt that hugged his chest become soaked in the steady stream of water.

"I called your name lass, you didn't answer."

"So you just decided to join me?" I tried to back away, but he gave a soft growl of warning and stepped in closer, not caring that he was now completely soaked from head to toe. And damn me if I didn't become ten times wetter with the sound.

"Aye, you were crying and," He looked down to where he'd trapped my hand against my pussy. "I thought maybe you were hurt." Dark grey orbs flicked back to mine, and I saw his pupils dilate with desire as his fingers began pressing my own against my clit again, moving them in slow circles. I had to swallow a moan and resist the urge to remove my hand to give him full access.

"Well, I'm not, so there's no reason for you to be here." My voice sounded low and throaty. Not at all how I intended.

He cocked his head slightly, a small smirk curling up one side of his full lips. "Oh, I think I have some very good reasons to be here." He nudged my fingers to the side even as he spoke, the thick pad of his thumb now pressing into my clit. "Reason number one. I don't know if I can trust you alone." I'd started to cut him off in outrage, but just then he slipped one finger deep inside me and I arched instinctively into his hand.

"Reason number two." He withdrew the first finger and then added a second as his hand pumped my pussy slowly. I bit my lip so hard to keep from moaning I thought I tasted blood. "I told you that I wasn't done tasting and learning every inch of your body. And I meant it. I don't know how much time we have, since you seem determined to stay, but I'm going to use every minute of it." His fingers curled inside of me, pumping a slow and steady rhythm, and I braced myself against the cold shower tile, trying to keep my legs from giving out from underneath me. He dipped his head then, capturing a nipple in his mouth and sucking on it with a groan. "Delicious. I can't get fucking enough, Hannah."

His silky voice curled around my ear as he kissed his way from my breast to my collarbone and then down the crease of my neck. His wet shirt chaffed against my skin and I tried to maneuver my hands so that I could pull it off, but he just pinned me harder to the tile.

"Do you want to know the third reason, lass?" He with drew his fingers just the edge of my opening, swirling them around, teasing me and I panted, nodding.

"I'll need your words, princess. Tell me what you want, Hannah." His thumb rubbed over my clit in slow, firm circles.

"I want your third finger, Simon, and then I want your cock." He chuckled and leaned down, his forehead touching mine.

"Och, you are a little she-devil. You'll get my cock, Hannah, just as soon as I get your release."

"The third reason, Si." I demanded, arching my hips into his hand, and his smirk deepened. This is what I needed. Whether or not he read my mind, or sensed the desperation of my desires, he was here and he was doing exactly what I wanted. Mostly. He eased two of his fingers back inside my channel partway and then withdrew again. I growled in annoyance.

"The third reason, lass, is because I want you to

know how wrong your sister is. You are the most incredible woman I've ever met. And you deserve to know." And then his third finger joined the other two and my pussy was convulsing around them as he rammed them hard inside of me. I couldn't speak, not only from the pleasure he was giving me, but from the words he spoke. Words that quieted the broken record of Sybil's voice I'd been playing on repeat ever since the showdown in Stockholm.

"Aye, that's it lass, come for me." He increased the pressure and pace, looking down to where his fingers were deep inside of me. "You're so beautiful when you come."

And then he dropped to his knees on the shower floor, still fully clothed, as he slung one of my legs over his shoulder, replacing his fingers with his mouth. His tongue swirled through my slick folds, tasting and capturing every bit of my arousal and release. I cried out, grinding against his mouth and then yanked on his hair, pulling him away from my core and bringing him up to my lips.

The kiss was nothing like we'd shared before. It was deep, full of feeling and with the taste of me on his lips, the most erotic thing I'd ever experienced.

With shaking hands, I fumbled with the wet opening of his jeans until he stepped back to assist me, pulling the soaked shirt over his head and dropping his pants to the shower floor. I had a moment to let my gaze travel over the healing bruises and cuts on his body and when I started to ask, concerned about his ribs again, he just shook his head. "Bruised, not broken. Got the clear from Evan this morning."

And then his lips and hands were on me again, hungry and demanding, yet tender at the same time. He hooked my leg around his waist before lining the tip of his erection against my opening, pausing for just a brief second. "Birth control?" The grip he maintained on his composure was herculean in effort, and the question cut through the fog of my lust for a moment. I nodded my head yes before rocking against him in consent. "Yes. Now Simon, *please.*"

It was the "please" that finally did it and with a groan that sent tingles all the way down my spine, he slammed home in one thrust. I had a brief moment to feel the fullness of him inside me, thicker, harder, than the teasing of his fingers from earlier before he was drawing back out and thrusting inside of me again. He set a punishing pace, not giving me a chance to catch my breath. Just waves of pleasure that built with every thrust until my entire body was screaming with the need for release. I briefly recognized my own voice crying out with a throaty, "Please, please, please."

"Aye, lass, I'll give you what you need." And then he was withdrawing to turn me around, kicking my legs out wide and forcing my body to bend so that I was arched, my hands braced against the shower wall. He entered me again, one hand gripping my hip tight, the other reaching around to strum delicately against my clit. "I've wanted to take ye like this ever since that day in yer interrogation room. Do ye remember, lass? When I pinned ye to the wall? Ye were a tigress and had yer claws sunk into me ever since."

I gasped. "I seem to remember it the other way around." A dark chuckle filled my ear, and he slammed into me, hard, dominating. "Aye, you had me pinned first, but now who's coming on my cock?" His fingers pinched my clit, and I saw stars. "That's it, princess, give it over to me."

My pussy fluttered, clamping down on the hardness that was filling me over and over again, squeezing and convulsing as the orgasm exploded through me. He cried out, gripping my hips with both hands now, his rhythm faltering and I felt him thicken as his release filled me. He stayed pressed against me, not pulling out or away, just holding me against him as his heart beat erratically against my back.

I closed my eyes, my own orgasm still sending shocks through my body. For a moment, we stayed that way, the steamy shower a momentary reprieve from the reality of our situation. But then the spell was broken, and he pulled away, leaning down to pick up his wet items. He gave my lips one last longing look before stepping out of the shower.

"We have the coordinates and the meeting time. We need to prepare."

And then he was gone, and so was my heart.

CHAPTER FIFTEEN

Hannah

Because of the location of Sergei's compound, in eastern Estonia just a few miles from the Russian border, we didn't have too far to travel from our hotel in Helsinki. Luckily, there wasn't a need for a helicopter flight this time as we intended to make our escape by boat. The compound itself was situated on a large island in the middle of Lake Peipus. It was a major shipping lane between the contested border between the two countries. A left over bygone of World War II and the fall of the Soviet Union.

The island was picturesque, with its single orthodox church and the few small businesses occupying the main village. There was only one bed-and-breakfast to accommodate any visitors or travelers, and it was obvious that the likely hood of that happening was few and far between. The most excitement this tiny island village ever got was a lost goat, or perhaps the occasional travel blogger who decided it would grace the populous with its presence in order to reveal the next big "hidden vacation gem". In reality, while pretty on the outside, the bleak history between Estonia and Russian aggression made most of the people less than welcoming of unfamiliar faces. They were more likely to slam a door in your face than risk any new business coming to town simply to keep the Russian wolves who smelled money in the water away from their door.

This made the area ripe for the picking for a man like Sergei Abromov. Someone who could play both sides of the fence like a fine tuned steel guitar and whose presence here would go unnoticed since it was so close to his own ancestral home. No one would look twice at his comings and goings. And no one would turn away the money he offered to keep it that way.

I glanced down at my watch for the millionth time and fidgeted in my seat. Even though technically I wasn't supposed to be raiding the compound with the rest of the team, they'd decided it was better to have me with them rather than back in Helsinki. I suspected it was more to monitor me more than anything, but I wasn't going to complain about it now.

They'd stuck me in a shabby little car that I was sure Micheal stole off some abandoned post Soviet Union car lot. When I'd started patting down the pockets of his jacket, he'd looked at me like I was crazy.

"What the hell are you looking for, Hannah?"

"Just checking to see if you have the keys to a Lexus or maybe a Range Rover stashed in there. You're like the Houdini of getaway cars, but I'm not sure this one is going to make it more than a few blown gaskets past the border guards."

Simon chuckled as he slide around to open the door for me and I shot Michael a pointed look when it'd screeched in rusty protest. "Your chariot, princess."

I rolled my eyes and slid across the cracked leather seat. The others followed suit, with Michael taking up his usual position as the driver. With Simon pressed to one side of me and Rue on the other, I still had my doubts and said so. "Honestly, I'm not sure how you guys expect us to get away in this pile of junk. We barely fit. Where's the terminator vehicle, Michael? There's no way you could have strapped a machine gun to the roof of this thing."

Michael's dark eyes just flashed with amusement as he slapped the dash, a plum of dust rising into the air. "Don't knock Betsy until you've tried her, Hannah.

Sometimes the biggest surprises come in the most unassuming packages."

I coughed, exaggerating the dust that filtered through the air, "Does Ole' Betsy come with an espestos warning?" but then sat back to take notice of our surroundings. We pulled away from the ferry that had brought us to the island and turned down a compact dirt road that wound through the hillside. The island was roughly seven kilometers in size and divided almost too neatly down the middle by a small river. The compound was apparently located at the northernmost point, between the banks of the river and a small inlet that led directly to the larger lake body.

Tactically, it made perfect sense. It would be unlikely that anyone would see any boats approaching the inlet and if they did, they would just assume they were fishermen. The river to its back and the short distance to the border made for an excellent egress route. We drove until Michael took a sudden turn off the main road onto a trail through the woods and I began to gain a small glimmer of respect for Betsy. She handled the rough terrain without falling apart at the seams.

No one spoke in the car, and for that, I was thankful. Even though technically I was only here to be overwatch and not at all allowed to engage. Something that Simon had made crystal fucking clear before we'd left.

"I mean it, lass. You'll not touch a weapon unless it's to save your ass and get out of there, or so help me god I'll tan it myself." He'd growled at me in that dark voice, leaving no room to argue.

I'd glared, "That's *your* kink, Si, not mine. And yeah, I got it. No playing the hero when you guys get your asses handed to you."

I'd tried once more to convince them it was a trap. To let them know that no matter how stealthy their approach, Sybil would no doubt be waiting for them. That was the thing with my sister. Everyone always saw her beauty and forgot about her brains. It's how she ensnared everyone she met into her sticky web. I'd watched the same thing play out with my parents when she'd so neatly hide the latest way she'd tormented me.

My new doll house defaced and covered in paint? It couldn't have been Sybil. Sybil would never be so careless with her paints. And look, not a drop on her dress. You're just clumsy, Hannah, you must have knocked it over. Oh Hannah, I'm so sorry you're sick sweetheart, now you can't go to your friend's house. What? Why would Sybil put something in your chili? You've just got a bad stomach bug. You'll be better by tomorrow, I'm sure. How could you say something like that about your sister?

I'd stopped complaining the day she'd murdered my puppy. I'd realized that nothing I said would ever be believed. And then all of a sudden, overt acts of maliciousness had stopped, but the subtle, more subconscious attacks stepped up. All the times Sybil had hinted that a boy I liked was out of my league. Or when my friends would come over and suddenly, I'd feel like I was on the outside of the group and Sybil would shine. The sun to their universe. And to mine. Even when she was making little comments and jokes at my expense, that everyone would laugh at. It got to the point where I'd stopped inviting my friends to hang out. Stopped going to other parties or doing anything with anyone outside of Sybil. And that's exactly what she'd wanted. *'You're MY Hannah. Isn't it so nice it's just us?"*

My stomach churned at the memories. So many times I'd just glossed over the way she'd treated me because that's what they had taught me to do. To ignore it and make excuses until my memories were nothing more than a confused jumble of fact and fiction. Once again, I thought back to my dad's phone call and then what Sybil had said right before she'd tried to kill me again.

"You have no idea what our mother and father did to me. Maybe instead of hunting me down, you should have started asking questions from dear old Mom and dad."

I frowned as we took another turn down what looked like a path barely wide enough for three people to walk down shoulder to shoulder, much less a car. But

Michael maneuvered old Betsy through the thick trees like he was threading a needle and I sighed with relief when we finally came to a stop outside of a crumbled down stone wall that marked the most southern part of the property. We were here, and it was time to put the thoughts of Sybil and our fucked up family dynamics to the side. But not for long, because no matter what happened next, I would definitely have a nice long chat with our parents. Like another one of Meema's phrases, "I was born at night, but not last night!". I may have been in the dark about Sybil, but I was about to shine the light on everything else.

CHAPTER SIXTEEN

Simon

I'd been observing Hannah's profile from my peripheral as Michael manipulated the rust bucket of a car through the rough back roads. Her accurate depiction of "Ole Betsy" had made me snicker. It was definitely a pile of junk, but I knew Michael had picked our transportation with one goal in mind and I trusted him to get it done.

The tantalizing scent of her jasmine and vanilla shampoo teased me and I'd had to adjust myself uncomfortably a few times during the short drive. Fortunately, she hadn't noticed, but I wondered what she would think if she happened to look over at the obvious bulge in my lap. When I'd caught her crying in the shower, I'd had no intention of fucking her, but when I'd glanced down to find her fingers seeking her own pleasure, all honorable thoughts had flown out the window. Then she'd opened eyes so filled with brokenness that I'd wanted to make that look disappear forever. To let her know, I saw her as she truly was. Beautiful. Intelligent. Loved.

That's why I'd left so quickly afterwards. I knew Hannah was a woman I'd never be able to get out of my system. It was more than lust fueled shower sex. Hannah could own me, heart, body and soul, if she wanted to. And she could destroy me just as quickly. The realization had me reeling, and I needed to get space as quickly as possible. I'd kept my distance during the mission prep, hiding behind the mask of professionalism I never seemed to be able to maintain for long around her. I could see the confusion and hurt in the quick glances she'd give me when she didn't think I was looking, but I couldn't let her know how dangerously close I was to falling. It had been agony. And now that we were confined in this small space, it was like every inch of me that was pressed to her was on fire with the desire to kiss the worried look on her face away.

I knew she was thinking about Sybil and I knew she

had no intention of staying put like I'd commanded of her. Only a fool would think that Hannah Kelly was going to let anyone keep her from getting to her sister. Hannah was single-minded when focused on a target, much like I was, but more than that, she wanted answers. Answers only Sybil could provide. I watched her drum her fingers nervously on her thigh and resisted the urge to capture her hand. As much as it killed me, this is where Hannah and I needed to part ways forever. Nothing good could come of us being together. And if that wasn't enough to convince her, then Sybil's death would.

We bumped along the barely there trail until we'd come to the broken down stone wall that hedged in the compound. During WWII, the island had been held a small outpost supplying arms to the Nazi resistance. As such, Nazi bombers nearly obliterated into obscurity it and all that remained of the old munitions building was this old wall. At least that's all that remained above ground. Below ground was another story, and that's where we'd find Sergei and his arms dealing contacts. I opened the car door and stepped out, making room for Rue and Hannah to follow. Michael, Evan and I would continue on foot from here to the main compound. Hannah and Rue would circle around to the eastern-most point of the property where a fisherman's boat had been moored by one of Michael's contacts. I wasn't going to ask him what additional promises he'd had to make to his family to make that happen, just noted that it would be one more debt to wipe from his ledger.

The plan was to get in, get Sybil and Sergei, plus any intel we could find and then make it back to the boat before Sergei had a chance to call in his reinforcements from the Russian side of the border. At least, that's what Hannah was told. I'd glossed over as much of the details as I could while making it sound as plausible as possible. She was far too intelligent for her own good and the way her green eyes had absorbed the map and the information told me she had suspicions of her own. But whatever thoughts she had, she didn't voice them. Just said we were idiots for thinking it wasn't a trap. Actually, her words had been, "You ain't got the sense god gave a billy-goat Simon Gallagher if you think this isn't a trap." Her southern drawl had somehow made the odd phrase sound even more insulting than if she'd told me to just fuck right off. It made me want to kiss her senseless.

I opened Ole Betsy's door, wincing at the way it creaked in protest, and climbed out, waiting for the others to join me. There was an old shed made up of half-rotted planks that was held together by moss and pure stubbornness. Evan shimmied inside and retrieved our gear that had been stashed there on a reconnaissance mission the day prior. After a few moments of pulling on body armor, checking weapons and coms, we were ready to go. If the weight of my kit felt heavier this time, I brushed it off as after effects from the long captivity. But a tingling feeling told me it had nothing to do with old injuries and everything to do with the weight I felt in my soul. Tonight, I'd finally complete the mission I'd been focused on ever since Victoria's death. I would shut the Abromov arms dealing down and Sybil Kelly would pay for what she did. Not just to me, but to Hannah.

I watched as Hannah and Rue slipped off into the dimness of the forest that surrounded us. We'd carefully planned the timing of their arrival at the boat around the security patrols that would be combing through the woods. No one would have expected us to arrive in the middle of the day and most of the security would be on higher alert once it got dark. It was just past dusk now, and we still had a few hours before it would be truly night. Then we could begin the carefully orchestrated dance of hunter and prey. I would have been lying if I didn't acknowledge that there was a dark part of me that enjoyed this part of my job the most, even if it was to seek my own revenge. Nothing mattered but the mission, and I could compartmentalize that above anything else. Still, I didn't take my eyes off Hannah's deliciously jean-clad backside until melted into the forest cover.

I felt more than heard Evan's presence as my side.

"You know she's not going to sit on that boat and just wait for us, right?"

I grunted and picked up my pack to sling it over my shoulders. "We can only hope she does. But if not, whatever she's got planned, we'll be done and gone before she can do anything." I looked at Michael, who was just scooting out from underneath Ole Betsy. He stood up and dusted his hands off his dark fatigues before accepting his own pack and weapon from Evan. He checked his gear over, methodical and meticulous, just like you'd expect from a former Special Ops soldier.

"You think Rue can really keep her from coming in to save her sister? I still think we should have left her back in Helsinki."

I gritted my teeth. That was the part of the plan that I'd spent agonizing hours tossing back and forth. I didn't trust Hannah by herself. Without a doubt, the hellion would have found a way to come with us, no matter what blocks we put in place. I also didn't trust that she wouldn't run right to her superiors and report on what we were up to. I trusted her handlers even less. So, even though I'd insisted she would stay behind, the plan had to be amended and that meant Rue was on babysitting duty.

"I think if anyone can talk sense into Hannah, it will be Rue."

Michael grinned, "I'm not sure who I feel sorry for the most right now. Hannah, Rue, or you."

"Me?" I shot him a look as we fell into step, circling around the wall in the opposite direction from where Hannah and Rue had left. "Why would you feel sorry for me?"

Evan snorted and smacked me on my back. "Mate, you don't see it, but we do. That little FBI agent has you wound up tighter than a hornet's nest, and when she realizes you tricked her again, she's going to have your balls for Christmas dinner. "

I glared. "This isn't up for discussion. Hannah will go back to the states and move on with her life. Our mission will be complete and then we can move on as well."

I ignored the look that Michael and Evan shared as I surged forward to take point. Night was falling fast, and we were close to coming up on our first obstacle. As I dropped my pack beneath against the branches of a wide tree, I flipped the communicator on and did a soft test of the mic, Michael and Evan doing the same. It was almost time for us to go radio silent and from now until the mission was complete, very few words would be spoken between us unless shit hit the fan.

Michael dropped to one knee beside me, his large hands moving over his own gear for one last check of everything. "What are we supposed to move on to after this, Simon?" His quiet question startled me, but I didn't say anything. "Will it be another mission? Another organization to take down? Another day crossing boundaries we aren't sure we want to cross? Making deals with ourselves that it's the right thing to do just so we can sleep at night?"

Anger flared, and I growled, "If you don't want to be on this team anymore, Michael, just say so. No one is holding you here."

It was his turn to growl back at me. "Wrong, you're holding us here, Simon. You and this fucking vigilante obsession you've had with Sybil ever since Victoria." He shoved a gloved, meaty finger into my chest and it took every ounce of control not to launch myself at him. But I had to remember this was Michael, not some stranger, mouthing off.

Evan's voice cut in before I could retaliate.

"Michael is right, Si." My jaw snapped shut in stunned silence. "Tory made her choices. She put her own greed and selfishness above you, above this team." He snorted and shook his head, a resigned look crossing his face. "She would have ended up dead no matter what. She would have made the same choices with or without you. Or me."

I stood up, anger vibrating through every inch of me. We had a mission to complete and standing here bickering over the whys and reasons would not change that. "So what, you two want to turn back? Go head back to the boat with Hannah and Rue, then. I'm here to do a job, and it's not done until I have Sergei and Sybil six feet under."

Evan's penetrating gaze pinned me to where I stood. "Do you hear yourself, Simon? You're willing to throw not only the one chance you've had at happiness in years away, but also the people who have stood by you for your revenge. Victoria was my fucking sister mate. But I never once blamed you or even Sybil for her death."

His words hit me like a punch in the gut. I couldn't form the words to respond. To tell them that my revenge had been all I'd held on to for so long, I didn't know if I could let it go. I didn't know who I was without it. But just then Rue's voice came in through the mic in our ears.

"Come in Reaper. Ghost Team Two is in place. Ready on your signal."

Evan and Michael stood in front of me expectantly, and I realized I had a choice to make.

I touched the communicator and flipped my nods

down, the night vision goggles casting everything around me in a green tinge. Michael and Evan did the same, and we began to move as one toward the compound.

"Roger that Ghost Team Two, Ghost Team One going silent. Reaper out."

And then we vanished into darkness, just like the operators we were. Like ghosts.

CHAPTER SEVENTEEN

Hannah

I kicked at a bucket that still stank of dead bait and grunted. Apparently, there wasn't anything on this island that wasn't rusted or half dead. If I thought Ole Betsy was bad, I was sure that this boat would have us either stranded or sunk before we even had a chance to get into open water. Noticing a couple of rusty metal boxes on the starboard side of the boat, I stepped around a few rotting ropes to give them a few quick kicks. Nothing but hollow metal rang back at me and I cursed.

"Did that box offend you?" Rue's playful voice called out to me and I turned to see the pretty woman pulling at the ends of a rope that looked much newer than the rest of the boat. The rope was wrapped around a black tarp covering a larger object, and since curiosity always got the best of me, I moved to help her.

"No, but this whole stinking operation does. And I'm not referring to the forty-year-old bait and traps over there. What happened to the all the flashy cars and sweet luxury tanks? Where's my Bond girl getaway speed boat?" I was deflecting. I'd been in pretty nasty stakeout locations over the years and this one didn't even rank middle grade compared to some others. What I really wanted to say was that I hated being stuck here in the back like some fragile, protected princess. *Like Sybil.* I wanted to know what was happening with the guys and if they had come across any trouble yet on their way to the compound.

I had this vision in my head of Sybil watching their approach on some giant big screen with a tank full of blood thirsty sharks swimming below her, just waiting to press the button and spring the trap that would drop the team to their deaths. Did I watch too many cheesy spy movies as a kid? Probably. Sybil wouldn't have a tank full of sharks anyway, because she didn't approve of cheesy movies. While anxiety gnawed at my stomach, I helped Rue tug the last of the ropes away.

She snickered, "Oui, I have asked myself the same question before. Being a spy has it perks, but more often that not it's just good ole' dirty work." She held onto the edge of the tarp and turned back to look at me with a twinkle in her eye. "And that is why I like my job the best." She paused for dramatic effect before sweeping the tarp away with one powerful tug. "While the boys play in the dirt, I get to play with the toys."

Beneath the tarp were several large, black, Tuff boxes and a few smaller pelican cases. I turned back to her and saw her looking at me expectantly, as if she'd just revealed some massive treasure of gold and was waiting for me to realize it was real and not fake. I blinked, and she just rolled her eyes and sighed. "It's all my tech Hannah, honestly, you're just like Simon. Evan at least pretends to be interested, if only because I find him all his dates."

It was my turn to snicker. "What about Michael? Does he like all your tech?" I drew tech out with a cocky grin and was rewarded with a blush as she handed me two of the smaller pelican cases.

"Michael actually taught me a lot about what I know now. He was my mentor of sorts when Simon first brought me on board the team." She began dragging one of the larger black boxes over towards the covered boat's cockpit and pushed open a rickety metal door. "I've always been good with programming and computers, but there was a big learning curve for a while."

I eyed her as she began popping open lids, pulling out portable tables and flipping open screens that seemed to appear out of nowhere. Portable battery packs were pulled from another box and then wires were plugged in with a smooth efficiency that spoke of someone who knew had done this repeatedly. Before I knew it, there was a small satellite dish scanning the sky, and we had a miniature intelligence skiff inside the dingy cockpit. She turned and grabbed the briefs from me as I stood there feeling like a complete fish out of water. Opening the cases, she pulled out two different laptops, one plugged in directly to the satellite dish, the other she opened up and after booting them up, logged into a program I didn't recognize. Not that I ever would. As I watched her fingers fly over her keyboard and a complicated stream of code appeared within a system of other codes, I realized that Rue might just be the coolest person I'd ever met.

The next thing I knew she'd let out a soft "Whoop!" and the laptop screen next to the satellite dish flashed and I was staring at an aerial overview of the island and Sergei's compound. It wasn't quite night-fall yet and so I could clearly see as vehicles approached the gates. An armed guard stepped out of a small guard shack and stopped them. Rue zoomed in and I tried to make out who occupied the vehicle, wondering if Sybil was in one of them or if she was already inside the compound. It was too hard to determine who it was though, and so I stepped back to allow Rue more room to maneuver.

"So now what?" I asked, when she zoned out for a few minutes, checking on her programs and switching through different monitor options. She was so focused that I must have startled her and she jumped slightly. "Now we wait. And if I see anything, I let the guys know. Once they get into position and get set up, I should be able to tap into their feed and we will see what they see."

I went to lean against one of the tables as her fingers continued to fly over her keyboard. "So we'll be able to see them as they approach the compound?"

She glanced up at me, amber eyes sparkling. "Better than that. We'll literally be able to see what they see." She did a few more taps, and a slit screen came up on the other laptop. I could now see the aerial view of the compound and but the other side was blank. Nodding to herself, she pulled out a headset and tapped a button.

"Come in Reaper. Ghost Team Two is in place. Ready on your signal."

I stiffened as I heard Simon's call sign. Reaper, as in the grim reaper. My heart raced, and I looked up at the darkening sky. Night was falling fast, and we were inching closer and closer to mission go time.

Simon's dark voice crackled over the coms and even though I couldn't hear all that he said, I shuddered at the chills it gave me. The next thing I knew, the blank screen flared to life, and I saw the forest where we'd left them illuminated in the green glow of night vision goggles.

I stood transfixed as I watched their dark figures bound from point to point towards the objective. The first obstacle would be to take out the guard gate without alerting the rest of the compound. A figure I recognized as Evan raised his hand, signaling them to stop. The camera stopped bobbing and shifted to a lower angle, and I realized that whoever we were watching had taken a knee. I could just make out the barrel of their weapon as they aimed it at an unknown target in the distance. I watched as another dark figure peeled off from the shadows, disappearing and then reappearing again around the back of the shack. Turning towards the other screen, I could see top down as the figure slipped inside the shack and for a few heart pounding moments there was nothing but silence.

Then the silence was broken with a sigh of relief as the same figure slipped back out, wiping off a knife that had the unmistakable signs of blood coating it, glinting in the light that illuminated the shack from within. My jaw clenched painfully with the tension. Rue was just as transfixed as I was, but she didn't seem as bothered by the obvious act of violence. Hadn't I known they were killers from the very first moment I'd met them?

"Reaper, you've got company approaching the inlet, moving fast."

I whipped around, so lost in my thoughts that I'd stopped paying attention to what Rue was doing and saw that she had the satellite imagery switched to monitoring the small inlet that led out to the lake. Sure enough, there were two speed boats skimming along the larger lake body, heading directly toward the compound. Tension gripped me and I leaned down to get a better look. The left side of the screen was continuing to move in the shadows of buildings as the team made its way toward the main building.

While Rue was watching the speedboats approaching, my focus was fully on the three mercenaries that crept in silence toward the small unassuming building that disguised the underground storage facility.

"Roger that. What's their ETA?" Simon's growly voice crackled through the headphones and my heart lurched.

Rue clicked a few buttons and zoomed out. The boats had just about crossed the lake and were almost to the mouth of the inlet. "Three minutes, maybe four. They're slowing down now."

"Do you have any idea who they are?"

Rue zoomed in to get a better view of the boats, but the chop of the water and the darkness made it nearly impossible to see. "No, I can't get a good look at the boat markings. It's too dark." She narrowed her eyes and leaned in closer. "Wait..."

Simon's voice cut in, "No time Rue, we can't be sure who it is. We're moving up the timeline."

"No, Si- wait..." But her voice was cut off as I slid behind her and brought the butt of my gun down on the back of her head and she slumped over, unconscious.

CHAPTER EIGHTEEN

Simon

For a moment I thought I'd heard Rue's faint voice in my ear but shook my head and signaled to Michael that it was time. He nodded and silently dropped to one knee, unslinging his pack and taking out a small radio transmitter. At the same time, Evan melted into the shadows and took up his position from a distance to scout out whoever was coming up behind us. I waited, slowing my breath and my heart rate down as I waited for the signal. In a few seconds, I had no doubt that the door would open and what remained of Sergei's guards would come streaming out of the building. I hoped that Sergei and Sybil would be in the mix, but I knew that was unlikely. They'd never expose themselves like that or risk their buyers' safety. Suddenly, the quiet night and my nods were lit with a large explosion and I closed my eyes against the glare for a brief second. Ole Betsy had done her job perfectly. For a moment, I wondered what Hannah would have done if she'd known that she'd been sitting directly on top of a moving bomb and couldn't help the slight grin that twitched at my lips. I could almost see her fury that would hide the underlying excitement from riding so close to the edge of chaos and danger. She was probably raging at Rue right now. There was no way half the island hadn't heard the bomb go off. I swallowed and pushed thoughts of Hannah away. I could hear distant shouting that sounded like it may be coming from the boats. They must have docked at the same time that Michael unleashed Betsy. I grinned darkly. Whoever it was probably hadn't been prepared for that. Good, until we knew who were dealing with I wanted them off their guard. But first things first, I had a target to take out. Just then, the door to the small warehouse burst open and a few confused and nervous guards spilled out, shouting in Russian. Michael and I moved as one, our bullets finding their targets with swift and final justice. It was over in seconds and as I stepped over the body of one guard; I frowned. Over in seconds and too easy. I looked at Michael and nodded back towards Evan, indicating that he should provide support should our boat friends be an issue. Nudging the door open, I took a quick glance around the small space. It was entirely empty other than a few folding chairs set near the door. In the center of the room, there was a set of stairs that descended into the underground storage facility. It was perhaps the most modern feature of the entire island, with the large opening lit on either side by dimly glowing led strips. I knew that there was this one entrance on the compound specs we'd received. But after carefully examining every bolt and concrete inch, discovered that there was also a hidden service elevator that led directly to a back exit that wasn't too far from where Hannah and Rue were docked. The plan was to take out Sergei and his buyers and then make our escape using the elevator and the boat. From there, we'd creep through the contested border waters as an Estonian fishing vessel until we hit a major port and our flight home. It was simple, really, until the unknown boats had shown up. I trusted Evan and Michael to take care of it, though, just like they trusted me to do what I had to do. Or did they? Their earlier words echoed in my mind as I crept down the stairs and approach a dimly lit hallway.

I approached the first locked room and paused, waiting to hear any movement, but it was quiet. I moved on to the next and found the same thing. Room after room down the long hall was quiet, and each door was locked. It looked like the information we'd received was correct and they used these first sets of rooms just for storage. Which meant that I was approaching the main meeting area, a larger open space that would be stacked with shelves of ammunition and weapons. And beyond that room would be the elevator.

Approaching a large double door, I paused, waiting to determine movement beyond it. But it was just eerily quiet. A gnawing worry formed. Few guards, quiet hallways, and I hadn't heard a peep from Rue or Hannah since the explosion. Nor had I heard anything from Michael or Evan letting me know the threat from the boats had been nullified. Fear, real genuine fear, surged through me and I burst through the doors, my weapon ready for whatever I would find beyond it.

But what met me was the last thing I'd ever expected. I stopped, every muscle in me vibrating with shock, confusion, and then fury. Because standing in-front of me, Sergei slumped to the ground next to her feet, with her gun drawn, was Hannah fucking Kelly.

She didn't say anything for a minute, her green eyes guarded and her face a calm mask.

"What are you doing here, lass?" I didn't lower my weapon. I saw Sergei but couldn't tell if he was alive or dead. There weren't any apparent signs of blood or trauma, but Sergei didn't move. Sybil was also nowhere to be seen, but that didn't mean that she wasn't somewhere nearby, ready to spring her trap.

"When you told me you'd had confirmation of Sergei's location and his next meeting with his dealers, it has sounded too good to be true." She looked down at Sergei and her lip curled up in disgust.

"I tried to tell you guys, but you were so dead set ongoing after him, you didn't want to listen." A guilty look flashed across her features. "I knew it was a trap."

"We went over this, Hannah." I growled, rage slowly building as I began to put the pieces together. "If we didn't go after them now, we might never get the chance again. It was a risk we took, and we planned for, carefully."

She nodded. "Yeah, you guys planned for everything. Everything but for Sybil doing what you'd never expect for her to do." Sadness filled her emerald green gaze. "I'm sorry, Simon, but this was the only way to fix things. David says there's always a choice, and he's right. But in this case, I really didn't have one. Sybil left me with no other options. It was the only way."

Once again, I was struck speechless, trying to understand what she was saying. What choice she didn't have?

I pointed to Sergei. "Lass, what did you do?"

"I didn't kill Sergei, if that's what you mean. He was like this when I got here." She frowned, "Sybil had to of done it. There's no way anyone would have gotten close enough." She shook her head and sighed, "Look, just tell Rue I'm sorry, ok? I did what I could and I promise that if you just trust me, everything will be alright."

Fear gripped me. "Hannah, what did you do? Where's Rue?" It hit me then that Rue wasn't with her and the lack of coms sent a stab of fear through me. "Ghost Team Two, come in, this is Reaper. Ghost Team One respond." I spoke into the mic but was greeted with nothing but silence.

I raised the barrel of my weapon and gripped it tighter. "Where's my team, Hannah?"

Hannah said nothing, just looked at me for a long moment, and I saw all the emotions she was feeling like a punch in my gut. I cleared my throat, "Hannah, lass, whatever this is. We can fix it. I promise, I dragged you into this. I will get you out of it."

Her features hardened with resolve, and she rolled her shoulders back. "That's what you don't get, Simon. I know you regret what you did to me. I also know you felt you had no choice, and I understand. But you're not the one who dragged me into this. Sybil did. She's been dragging me behind her for years. But I'm done playing by her games."

I dropped my weapon and moved towards her.

"Hannah, you don't have to play by anyone's games.

Sergei's dead, Sybil has fled apparently. Whatever trap she tried to spring, it hasn't worked."

She looked up at me, green eyes searching mine for a moment before she leaned up and pressed her lips to mine. The kiss startled me for a brief moment, but before I even had the chance to kiss her back, she pulled away from me.

"That's where you're wrong, Simon. The trap worked." She squared her shoulders again, and for the second time since I'd met her, pointed her weapon directly at my head. "Simon Gallaher, you are under arrest for the murder of Simeon Sergei Abromov and interference in an international operation to apprehend a known terrorist suspect."

Just then, I heard the double doors open behind me and a voice I had not heard in years grated on my ears.

"Excellent work Agent Hannah, we will take it from here. Mr. Gallagher, if you would please drop your weapon and place your hands on top of your head."

I watched as Hannah backed slowly away from me, never dropping her weapon. I couldn't look away from her. The entire room seemed to suddenly narrow down to nothing but the few short paces between us. And suddenly I understood everything. This was the trap that Sybil had sprung. And she'd used the one person I had not expected against me to do it.

Hannah's eyes seemed to convey a message, but

what it was, I didn't care to know anymore. Everything was coming around full circle and I could finally see the truth. Hannah and Sybil might as well have been the same person. I didn't flinch or resist when I felt large hands pat me down and confiscate my weapons.

"Are you listening Mr. Gallagher? Do you understand the charges brought against you?" Agent Reed's voice made my lip snarl, and yet I didn't tear my gaze away from Hannah.

"When did they let you out to do an actual agent's work, Frank?"

Agent Reed's thin lip curled up in disdain and I couldn't help but feel some small satisfaction as shock registered in Hannah's eyes. Oh yes, little hellcat, you're about to uncover a lot of ugly truths.

"That's enough from you Mr. Gallagher. I've been waiting a long time for this moment and finally, we have enough evidence and testimony," He smiled, sickeningly, at Hannah, and damn me if I didn't want to rip his eyeballs out of his head for daring to look at her like that. "From the lovely Agent Kelly. I'd say her hard work has earned her a promotion." He licked his lips, and I added his tongue to the list of body parts I wanted to remove from him. "Wouldn't you say so, Agent Kelly?"

Hannah looked mildly disgusted and slightly annoyed. "I'd say I've earned at least a week-long nap and my job back. But thank you, Agent Reed." She added as almost an afterthought, and I tried not to be pleased with her fire.

"Where's my team?" I watched as a few Interpol agents knelt to examine Sergei's body as another agent turned me around, leading me back up the hallway I'd just come down.

"They're currently being processed and detained for questioning in a recent string of international crimes and espionage." Agent Reed's nasally voice irritated my eardrums, and it took everything in me to not lean forward and bash my skull against his. My control was quickly slipping.

I looked at Hannah. "Who is being detained, exactly?" She shook her head slightly, trying to convey something, but Agent Reed interrupted our silent conversation with a wave of his hand and continued on as if he hadn't heard my question.

"One of your friends seems to have even more unsavory connections than you do. His family has already had a lawyer calling my office non-stop for the past week, demanding we dismiss any investigations or charges brought against him. Your childhood mate, however, will probably be sent back to the United Kingdom to answer for some of his war crime charges there. As for the infamous Fleur de lis, I'm sure it's just a matter of time before she is in custody as well and will answer for her trophy of cyber crimes."

A slight weight lifted from me. They hadn't gotten to Rue yet. I looked at Hannah and tried to convey my thanks. She'd betrayed us, but had made sure Rue was kept safe.

As we approached the entrance to the underground building, I cast one last look at her. I took note of everything. The mess of brunette hair that spilled over her shoulders. The way her dark shirt and cargo pants hugged her curves. Her eyes were a bright green with sadness and regret. Before they dragged me through the doors, I paused, forcing the agents escorting me to stop short.

"I wasn't going to kill Sybil Hannah. No matter what happens, I needed you to know that. I would not kill her."

She gasped slightly in shock at my confession, but said nothing as they dragged me toward the docks and boats that were waiting to take me away. And I didn't look back.

Hannah

"You got it?" Anxiety gripped me and I tried not to let it show in my voice as I waited for the response on the other end of the line.

David's low voice answered after a brief hesitation. "Yeah, I got it."

"Thank god." I sighed with relief and let go of my Saint Michael's pendant, the gold chain nearly an imprint in the palm of my hand.

"Hannah, this is it. I can't do anything more for you now. I have to look after my own career and family."

Guilt flooded me. "I know David. I promise, I'm not asking for anything else. After this, I'm done."

"Are you sure you want to do this? Your whole

career, your life, your family. You'll be giving it all up."

I swallowed thickly, emotion building and I looked down at the gravel path I was standing on, my hot pink converse a clash of color against the brown and gray.

"I've never been more sure of anything in my life, David."

He cleared his throat and I could picture him rubbing a large hand down his face in frustration and worry. "You know there's no guarantee this will work, or that you're not going to end up in the same place he is."

I bit my lip, nudging a rock with my toe. "I know, but I have to try."

He sighed and didn't say anything for a moment. "Well," his voice was thick with emotion as well when he responded, "This is goodbye then. Good luck, kid."

"Goodbye, David." I didn't say thank you for what he did, or the risks he took. It would have just pissed him off. My thanks to him would be to make sure the plan didn't fail.

I looked up at the small country home in the distance and my resolve firmed.

And step number one to that plan? Get some fucking answers.

I shoved my phone in my pocket as my feet carried me toward my parents home. It was time for dear old Mom and Dad to start answering some questions.

Thank you so much for joining me on this journey! As a self-published author your reviews are so helpful and I'm so thankful for them. Authors, proof readers, and editors are only human! So please, if you see an error or have any questions, email me at authoranneroman@gmail.com

Thank you! Xoxo- Anne

ACKNOWLEDGMENTS

To my family and friends who support me on this journey, thank you!!

To my readers who encourage me to continue and want to read the stories I have to tell, there are not enough thanks in the world.

To my ARC readers- you are amazing and so badass. I couldn't do it without you!

And to my friend Christine who planted the seed to begin with, one day I promise to write that espionage thriller for you!

Most importantly, to my husband Z. Your love and encouragement is what keeps me pushing. Thank you for always believing in me.

Xoxo- Anne

Anne Roman is a busy mother of four kids, two cats, and one super cute puppy. When she's not running around like a mad woman to and from sporting events or school activities, she's trying to get the stories in her head down on paper. Luckily she has an amazing husband who is always ready with coffee, wine, and a hug.

Dangerous Entanglements Trilogy

See Me

Find Me

Coming Soon!

Catch Me

DE
CATCH
Me
DANGEROUS ENTANGLEMENTS: BOOK THREE
ANNE ROMAN